THE ARTISTS OF WOODBRIDGE

Isla Milne intends to stay with her relatives in Woodbridge only until she has put her life back in order. But then she meets a group of local artists, amongst them talented sculptor Jed Rowley. Soon she becomes integrated in village life and involved with the summer school at Rowley Grange, and things take on an interesting dimension as she builds new and discovers old connections in the area. Meanwhile, Isla finds herself becoming increasingly attracted to Jed — but he is already dating the glamourous and possessive Nicole . . .

JEAN M. LONG

THE ARTISTS OF WOODBRIDGE

Complete and Unabridged

LINFORD
Leicester

First published in Great Britain in 2020

First Linford Edition
published 2020

A catalogue record for this book is available
from the British Library.

ISBN 978–1–4448–4522–8

Published by
Ulverscroft Limited
Anstey, Leicestershire

Set by Words & Graphics Ltd.
Anstey, Leicestershire
Printed and bound in Great Britain by
T. J. International Ltd., Padstow, Cornwall

This book is printed on acid-free paper

1

Ellen stared at her niece intently. 'So, what do you think of that for a plan?' she asked, looking pleased with herself.

Isla was momentarily rendered speechless. She had had a busy day packing up the remainder of her possessions, piling them into the back of her small car and checking that Gran's house was left how she would wish it to be, before visiting the elderly lady for a short time in the residential home. Having satisfied herself that her grandmother really was settling in, she had driven from Bexhill-on-Sea to Kent.

'Well?' Ellen was getting impatient.

Isla swallowed. 'I hadn't expected the house to be sold so soon and my possessions relegated to a pile of cardboard boxes!'

Ellen raised her cool, grey eyes skywards. 'Don't be so melodramatic, Isla!

You've already said that Kate and Matt don't mind how long your stuff is stored in their garage.'

'No, but I don't want to take advantage.'

Ellen sighed. 'We're offering you a home here, just until you get on your feet. You must see it from our angle. We couldn't turn down a cash offer — not when my mother is going to need the money to fund her residential care.'

Isla swallowed. 'No, I appreciate that, but it's all happened so quickly that I've not had a chance to get my head round it. OK, so just let me see if I've got this right. You and John are going to New Zealand to his niece's wedding and want to stay on for a while after that to do some sightseeing.'

'Got it in one! You can stay here to keep an eye on the house and John's workshop, and that will give you time to do some painting. So, what do you say?'

Isla, who had had a few plans of her own, realised that, in the circumstances, there wasn't much she could say.

Someone needed to be around for Gran, even if she was safely settled in a home. Isla was just going to have to put her own plans on hold for a while longer.

She nodded, 'OK — but you do realise I'll need to find some work for the autumn. I haven't had the opportunity to do anything about it yet, but now that Gran's in a home, the carer's allowance has been stopped.'

'Naturally. Well, you won't need to pay any rent whilst you're here and we can pay you a little to keep things ticking over in the workshop. And, then, of course, there's the summer school at Rowley Grange.'

Isla frowned. 'Yes, about that . . . '

'Oh, John will fill you in when he gets back. He's got a proposition to put to you too, but that's going to have to wait because, right now, we need to get organised for the Open Art Studios tomorrow. Anyway, we'd better have some supper first. I'm afraid it's only quiche and salad, but I'll cook some

3

new potatoes. Whilst I'm getting it ready, why don't you go upstairs and unpack some of your things?'

Upstairs in the pleasant but rather austere bedroom, Isla sank onto the bed and wondered what the future held. Just over a year ago, she had been working full-time at the local college where she'd taught art. She had rented a flat near her work, had a steady boyfriend and the future looked rosy. But then Gran's health had deteriorated, and she'd needed more and more help. Isla could have wished that Ellen and John had been around a bit more for Gran, but she knew they led busy lives; she had to accept the situation and not be selfish.

Isla's grandparents had brought her up since the age of twelve when her mother, Ellen's sister, had died in a helicopter crash. Isla had never known who her father was, and, nor it seemed, had anyone else in the rest of her small family.

Finally, Isla had decided that her best

option would be to work part-time. After a few months, she'd reluctantly given in her notice, moved in with Gran, and taken on the role of carer. Ewan hadn't understood, and after a short while, they had had a bitter row and parted company.

On reflection, Isla realised it was for the best. They had been drifting for a while, and she knew she could never marry someone who showed so little empathy. He wasn't the person she thought he was.

After a short while, her grandmother decided to sell up and move into a residential home so that Isla could get on with her life.

'A couple of my friends are there already and it seems a nice place, so you've no need to worry, love,' the elderly lady had assured her.

Once Gran had made up her mind, there was no talking her out of it. Reluctantly, Isla had agreed, hoping fervently that her grandmother had made the right decision.

'Supper's ready!' Ellen shouted up the stairs, and Isla hastily tidied herself up.

'Aren't we waiting for John?' she asked, entering Ellen's state of the art kitchen a few minutes later.

Ellen shook her head. 'He's rung to say he's stuck in a traffic jam.'

Over the meal, Isla broached the subject of her own paintings. 'I've got a selection of my work in the back of the van. Am I going to display it here?'

Ellen looked surprised. 'What made you think you were going to do that?'

Isla was taken aback. 'Because, when I spoke on the phone with John, he suggested I brought the paintings along. I thought they would be displayed here in the cottage.'

Her aunt frowned. 'But you're not a member of any of the local groups, are you?'

'Well, no, but I assumed that as I was going to be involved in village affairs, it would be a good introduction. John obviously thought the same.'

'Hmm — well John can sometimes be a bit of a law unto himself. Oh, you'll have to sort it out with him when he gets in but, as you can see, there's absolutely no space here.'

Isla felt disappointed. She ought to be used to her Aunt Ellen's forthright manner after all these years, but this still came as a blow. She'd hoped that having been out of work for several months, she might be able to get back on her feet again. She'd had high hopes of the artists' open weekends being a means of promoting her work.

Ellen busied herself by clearing the plates. 'I haven't made a dessert but there's fresh fruit and yoghurt and then, after coffee, we'll need to press on.'

They were drinking coffee when John finally arrived with a couple of local artists close on his heels, who had come to set up their displays.

John was one of Isla's favourite people in the whole world. The two of them got on like a house on fire. He was the complete opposite of Ellen — easy going, untidy and very positive.

He sat down at the kitchen table and devoured his meal hungrily. 'Yes, of course I said Isla could display her work.' He said in answer to Ellen's question. 'I've enrolled her as an associate member of the group.'

Ellen raised her pencilled eyebrows. 'Then I hope, for your sake, you've run it past Jed Rowley,' she warned him.

'I don't want to cause any problems,' Isla told them uncomfortably. Things were not turning out as she'd imagined.

'You won't,' John assured her cheerfully. 'Look, why don't you go down to my workshop now whilst the light's still good? That's where you're going to display your paintings. I'll follow on when I've finished my meal.'

Ellen looked disapprovingly at her husband. 'Be it on your own head,' she told him direly, and went to open the door to another member of the group.

'She's a bit under pressure,' John said, running his fingers through his

8

dishevelled mop of greying hair. 'It's the first time we've opened our cottage for these artists' open weekends. Ellen's a bit of a perfectionist, as I'm sure you're aware; she's worked herself into the ground to get everything looking just so.'

'Could you explain where this workshop of yours is?' Isla implored, anxious to get her paintings sorted out.

'Oh, haven't you been there before?'

'Actually, no. After all, you haven't lived here that long, have you? On the one or two occasions I visited with Gran, we came for Sunday lunch, if you remember, and then went home mid-afternoon. We didn't get to look around and anyway, Gran couldn't have walked too far. Usually, you came to Bexhill or we met you halfway at a pub.'

John looked uncomfortable. 'Yes, well, we thought it was easier for Ellen's mother — what with the journey and everything.'

Isla wasn't too sure what the *everything* was, and suspected it was probably Ellen making excuses. Since Isla's grandfather had died a few years back, Ellen and Gran seemed to have had an uneasy relationship. Isla had never been able to establish why, because her grandmother avoided the subject.

John got up and went with her to the door of the cottage.

'You turn into the lane, go past the cottages and, after a few minutes, you'll see a track leading down beyond the church and the vicarage.' He waved his arm in the general direction. 'The workshops are in a converted stable block that used to belong to the manor house . . . Wait a minute, you'll need the key.'

He disappeared into the study and emerged holding a large key.

'It's the third door along. Beyond that is the barn where the WI will be serving refreshments. I expect they'll be setting things up now. They're a friendly crowd. It'll be good for you to get acquainted with them. Anyway, if you take a look to see if I've cleared enough wall space for you, I'll be along presently. I expect you'll need a hand with hanging your paintings.'

'Where do I park?' she asked.

'Oh, you go ahead on foot. It's only a short walk. I'll bring your work along with the rest of mine in the van. It's a good opportunity for you to suss out the locality.'

'OK,' she said uncertainly. Her paintings were still in the boot of her car and she and John transferred them to his van.

'So, who exactly is this Jed Rowley?' she wanted to know. 'Is he related to the Jerome Rowley who interviewed me on Skype about the summer school?'

'His son. Jed's a nice chap, although he comes across as a bit authoritative at times. Lives at Rowley Grange. You'll pass it on the way. He's responsible for organising the open day,' John told her vaguely.

'Right. Then let's hope he doesn't put in an appearance and veto what I'm doing, or I'll be wasting my time, won't I?'

Finally, she set off, leaving John to finish his meal in peace. Turning into a narrow lane, she saw the spire of the church ahead. She looked around her with interest. There was a little stream running beside the road; wildflowers bloomed in profusion on the grass verge.

She took a deep breath. For the first time that day she had time to gather her thoughts. Perhaps it wasn't a bad idea to make a completely fresh start away from Bexhill and her past life. Once John and Ellen had gone to New Zealand, she'd have time to think about her future.

On her left, she saw a row of cottages, their gardens a riot of colour, and then a large, Georgian vicarage close to the church. Nearby was another red brick building which looked like a village hall. Beyond was a driveway with a sign which read: Rowley Grange. The name rang a bell and she realised it was where the summer school would be taking place in a few weeks' time.

A moment later Isla stopped and stared at another sign which pointed to Hawthorne Manor, a nursing and residential home. Her grandmother could have come here to be near her family.

Isla swallowed hard. Ellen hadn't mentioned that there was a home just a short distance away from where she lived. Sadly, she could only conclude that it was because Aunt Ellen had obviously had no intention of having her mother living too near to her.

Isla found the track easily enough, and a few minutes later she came across what was obviously the stable block. Beyond was the barn, where she could see signs of activity. She struggled with the key and eventually the door swung open. It was a small, compact area that was perfect for John's pottery.

Isla stood gazing around her at the whitewashed walls. There were several wall boards, all waiting for her to display her paintings on them.

She wandered round, looking at John's pottery in its muted shades of blues and greens, cream and brown. She'd known he was talented but had never seen an entire exhibition of his before. There were a selection of jugs, vases and bowls, but her attention was caught by the delicate ceramic figurines in a glass showcase. She stooped to take a closer look. The door creaked open and she supposed it was John.

'May I ask what you're doing here? We're not open to the public until tomorrow morning. How did you get in?' demanded a curt voice.

Startled, Isla swung round. The man who had challenged her was tall and broad-shouldered, with lean features, thick fair hair and piercing sea-green eyes. She met his gaze levelly, even though her heart was beating rapidly.

'John Ainsworth gave me the key; I'm displaying some of my work here tomorrow.'

'I don't think so. The exhibitions are

for local members only,' he said coolly. 'Anyway, who are you — one of John's students?'

'No. I'm his niece by marriage — Isla Milne. Ellen Ainsworth is my aunt,' she informed him.

He frowned. 'So why on earth would John think *that* relationship would entitle you to exhibit your work alongside the rest of us, I wonder.'

Isla returned his gaze steadily from rich brown eyes. 'You'd better ask him. He'll be along shortly. But, for your information, I've been accepted as an associate member of the society.'

His eyebrows shot up as he stared at her incredulously. 'You've been accepted as what? You must be mistaken. There's no such thing as an *associate member*, I'm afraid.'

'And who are you to dispute it?' she asked indignantly, but even before he replied she knew the answer.

He stood there, hands on hips, fixing her with a penetrating stare from stormy green eyes. 'I'm Jed Rowley,' he told her, 'and before you ask, I'm in charge of this whole shebang.'

There was an uncomfortable pause and, just in time, John arrived with an armful of Isla's paintings.

'Evening, Jed. I see you two have met then,' he remarked unnecessarily.

'It would seem so,' Jed Rowley replied coolly. 'Who exactly led you to understand that your — er — niece could become an associate member in order to exhibit her paintings during the open days?'

'Actually, it was your father,' John told him, carefully setting down Isla's paintings against the back wall.

'I see,' Jed said, in a voice that told them he didn't see at all. 'Then I'd best take the matter up with him.'

John nodded and carried on with his task. The door closed with a bang.

'That went well!' Isla commented, a sinking feeling in the pit of her stomach. 'Are you sure I ought to be displaying my paintings? I don't want to cause bad feeling.'

'Oh, take no notice of Jed. He's probably had a bad day at work. I've run it past Jerome Rowley and that'll be enough to satisfy the rest of the committee.'

John was studying her paintings. She'd selected some of her watercolours — mainly landscapes. A number of them depicted scenes of the Lake District, where she'd spent several delightful holidays.

'These are really good, Isla — amazing, in fact. How come I haven't seen any of them before?'

'Well, actually, you would have seen one or two on the walls at Gran's house, but most of them were at the college or stashed in the attic.'

'You've been hiding your light under a bushel.'

Isla felt a warm glow inside her. Praise from John was praise indeed! She valued his opinion, knowing that, even though he now specialized in pottery, he was also an experienced artist himself.

'Now, are you happy for them to be

17

hung straight onto these white display boards or do you want some backing material?'

Isla considered. 'What do you think?'

'If you want my opinion, I'd be inclined to put them straight onto the white. Sort them into groups and I'll hang them up for you. I've just got to finish arranging my own stuff.'

'I love those subtle colours, John. Gran's taken the fruit bowl you made her for Christmas to the home. I do so hope she's going to be happy there.'

'It was her choice to go in a home, love. No-one forced her and she has got a couple of friends there already.'

'I know, but it's not the same, is it, as being in your own home.' Isla said worriedly. I hadn't realised there was a residential home near here. I wonder if she knew.'

For a moment John didn't reply. He rearranged some of his pottery, added a few pieces to it, and then he turned to face her, looking serious.

'Your grandmother is still capable of

making her own decision
fancied going into that
Bexhill, and once she'd *
up there was no stopp:
in his reasonable way. 'W:
not have realised is that u
difficult transferring someone o1
advancing years from one county to
another. There's all the medical stuff to
sort out for a start — quite apart from
the financial matters.'

'Yes, I suppose so.' Isla decided it was
best not to pursue the matter any
further. It was, after all, her grandmother's choice. Despite her frail body, she
was still perfectly *compos mentis*, and
as John had pointed out, quite able to
make up her own mind; although she
had left the sale of the house and the
disposal of the bulk of the contents to
Ellen and John.

After a few minutes, John began to
hang the dozen or so pictures Isla had
selected for the exhibition and the
conversation reverted back to the open
weekend.

'k off is at eleven,' he told her as
bk another painting from her. 'The
n will be open shortly before then
r refreshments. There are to be other
vents around the village. There are
tours of the church tower and exhibitions in the barn. I must introduce you
to the vicar — he's very supportive.'

'You obviously like living here.'

'Yes — well, I was raised in the
country and the rural life suits me far
better than London.'

'And Aunt Ellen?'

'Oh, she's got plenty to keep her
occupied — she's near enough to the
leisure centre and she's joined a few
local groups. It's quite an affluent area
and she can still get up to London to
visit her friends or go to the theatre.'

John concentrated on hanging the
pictures for a few minutes.

'I expect you're looking forward to
your trip to New Zealand?' Isla asked,
as he straightened the last one.

'Can't wait. Last time I went there was
for my cousin's funeral. Ellen couldn't

come because she was finishing a project for some wealthy, influential clients. Now that she's not working it makes things easier.'

He climbed down and surveyed his handiwork. 'How's that?'

'Brilliant! Thanks John. You've made a much better job than I would have done.'

'We make a good team, don't we? And Isla — don't worry about Jed Rowley or anybody else who questions your associate membership. I've cleared it with Jerome Rowley so, as far as I'm concerned, that's all that matters.'

A memory of Jed Rowley's penetrating green eyes and arrogant manner came into Isla's mind and she just hoped John was right.

2

Isla awakened to a bright, sunny morning. She showered and dressed quickly in a denim skirt and white T-shirt. She still hadn't had the opportunity to unpack anything other than the essentials and felt a bit apprehensive about the day ahead.

Breakfast was a sketchy affair as Ellen was anxious to get on. Isla's cereal bowl was whisked away almost before she'd finished her muesli. She grabbed her mug of tea before it suffered the same fate.

John struggled past her, carrying several garden chairs and a piece of toast firmly clenched between his teeth. He gave her a meaningful wink.

'So, what would you like me to do, Ellen?' Isla asked after she'd cleared the table.

Ellen picked up a sheet of paper from

the table. 'Oh, just let me check the rota . . . Right, I shall need you here by two o'clock to help out. You'd better go off with John this morning I suppose, seeing as Jerome Rowley's apparently sanctioned your associate member status — although that's news to me. John has this infuriating habit of forgetting to tell me things.'

'Perhaps I can take a look round at the displays first,' Isla suggested. 'After all, if I'm going to help out then I need to know what's here, and there wasn't time last night.'

'Yes, well, make it quick before the others get here. Oh, and you can take a few of the booklets and other leaflets down to the workshop in case John forgets.'

Isla peered through the kitchen window into the garden, where John and another man were busily putting up gaily coloured umbrellas over the tables beneath a striped awning.

'Are you serving refreshments here as well?'

'Just soft drinks, tea, coffee and biscuits. Some people might like to sit in the garden for a little while.'

'It's a lovely garden, Ellen. I shall enjoy looking after it whilst you're away.'

'Oh, we can discuss all that later. Off you go, then.'

Isla hesitated in the doorway. 'What about you?'

'What about me?' Ellen looked startled.

'John said you'd be exhibiting some of your own work. Whereabouts is it?'

Ellen's attractive features relaxed. 'In the dining-room — just a few examples of my design and textiles which I thought might be of interest. Oh, come on, I might as well show you. We're more or less ready and it's barely nine o'clock. My friend Jane's husband, Alan, is lending a hand with the garden furniture, as you can see.'

Ellen was very talented; Isla had always known that. Her aunt had trained at the same art college as John, but when they'd qualified, they'd gone their own separate ways for a number of years. She'd had a highly skilled job in design and textiles, creating wallpaper and soft furnishings for people who had money to throw about.

Isla stood surveying the exquisite cushion covers, draped fabrics and the framed wallpaper designs, some in striking contemporary patterns. The centrepiece was an amazing quilt patchwork in black and white with appliqué and delicate embroidery.

'You are gifted, Ellen,' she said admiringly.

'Oh, it's all so much easier now, since computers arrived on the scene. I haven't produced anything fresh for this exhibition. This is work I had previously. I don't know quite how I got press-ganged into taking part in these open weekends. A few months ago, John asked me to help him with a talk he was giving to one of the local groups and it escalated from there.

'Anyway, enough of me. There's a lot

of talent within the group and you need to look at some of the other exhibits, both here and at the other venues. The variety is amazing — '

Ellen broke off as the doorbell pealed. John had got there before her, and a couple of minutes later two women came into the room.

'This is my niece, Isla Milne; she is going to be living here for a while. Isla — this is Jane Bradshaw and her daughter, Amy. Jane is a silversmith and Amy has produced some wonderful glass work.'

Isla would have loved to have lingered but sensed that John was itching to get to his workshop, and so after a moment or two they left.

'How does the thought of a bacon sarnie grab you?' he asked, as they set off along the track.

Isla grinned, 'Wonderfully naughty. Why? Is there somewhere we can buy one?'

'Yes — the bakers down the high street. The WI can't oblige as they'll be too busy with cakes and scones for when they open at ten thirty. There are always a few early-comers.'

'So, you want me to do some sneaky shopping?'

'Absolutely. I'm starving and Ellen doesn't keep bacon in the house — says it's not healthy.' He patted his stomach. 'One slice of toast and a bowl of granola, or whatever it was, is hardly going to keep me going.'

He pulled in along the lane and handed her a five-pound note and some loose change. 'I'll park the van and then I'll put the kettle on!'

Isla found the bakers with no problem and joined the queue. She found herself standing next to Amy Bradshaw.

'Don't tell me,' Amy grinned, 'you're suffering from breakfast withdrawal symptoms too!'

Isla smiled back. 'Yes, but this is a state secret.' She put a finger to her lips.

Amy grinned. 'Same here. I've escaped for a bit. Told Mum I wanted to look at some of the other exhibits whilst I'd got the opportunity and promised on pain of death to be back before eleven. Mum says you're exhibiting too. How come?'

Isla found herself explaining yet again. 'What about you?'

'Me? Oh, I've got a few pieces dotted about — nothing mega. I'm a bit busy this year running courses and preparing my students at school for their A levels.'

This captured Isla's interest, but before she could ask any more questions it was her turn to be served. She waited until Amy had made her purchase. The pair of them gathered up their paper bags and left the shop.

'Why don't you come down to the workshop? John's put the kettle on,' Isla invited. 'You can have a quick peek at his pottery.'

'Brilliant — then I'll have a clear conscience about this,' she indicated the bag. 'So are your exhibits in John's workshop?'

Isla nodded. 'Just a handful of

paintings. Are yours at Ivy Cottage?'

'A few. I work in mixed media, but this year I'm showing some of my efforts made from glass: dreamcatchers, et cetera.'

'Really?' She wrinkled her brow trying to visualise the exhibits she'd seen that morning. 'I saw some of the things at the cottage including Ellen's textiles, but don't remember any glasswork.'

Amy shrugged. 'Yes, well — to show them to their best advantage they need light behind them, but your Aunt Ellen didn't seem too keen to have them on the windows, or come to that, in her garden. There are a few pieces in the conservatory, but I've taken the rest to one of the other venues — Gardenia House. It's actually better there because they've got artificial light inside a display cabinet, and a gorgeous garden for my garden glass ornaments.'

There was an uncomfortable pause, which Isla broke by saying, 'I'm feeling awkward because I've caused a bit of a problem with some guy called Jed Rowley over this so-called *associate membership* that's been granted me by his father. I don't understand why Jed's in charge when his father seems to have quite a lot of authority.'

'Oh, that's easily explained: it's because Jed has taken over from his father this year. Jerome was ill back in the autumn. The open weekends were his baby originally; he was the brains behind the whole thing. He's brilliant at organising things and has a lot of influence. He's been very generous both with his time and money but has had to step back for the time being — only he doesn't like relinquishing the reins completely.'

'Right. Oh, well, I suppose I'll just have to see how things work out,' Isla said.

'So, what made you decide to escape to the country?' Amy asked, as they approached the workshops.

'Ellen's mother — my grandmother, moved into a residential home and, as

I'd been living with her and the house was being sold, I had to move on.'

She braced herself for the inevitable question about a husband or partner, but to her relief John spotted them at that moment from the window and ushered them inside.

The forbidden breakfast was equally as delicious as it smelt and, whilst they ate, John filled them in with what he would be doing that morning in the way of demonstrations, explaining that Isla could wander round some of the other venues whilst that was happening.

As Isla rinsed her greasy fingers at the small sink in a corner of the room, she reflected that the morning was already turning out to be more pleasant than she had expected.

Several of the helpers from the barn popped in before eleven to take a quick look at John and Isla's exhibits. 'You're such a gifted family,' a middle-aged lady was remarking, when the door opened, and a scholarly grey-haired gentleman came into the workshop.

After exchanging a few words with the volunteers, he came to stand beside them.

'Good morning, John — and I take it this is your niece?'

'Yes, this is Isla Milne. Isla, this is Jerome Rowley.'

'Ah, we meet in the flesh at last.' He extended his hand. 'Those darned video set-ups are never the same, are they?'

Isla smiled, remembering the very informal conversation they had had a short while back. 'No, they can take some getting used to. Nice to meet you, Mr Rowley.'

Through the window she could see Jed Rowley speaking with a group of visitors, and a moment or two later he came into the workshop.

'I gather you've met my son already?' Jerome said.

Isla nodded, aware that Jed was viewing her with a resigned look, and deliberately not meeting his eyes.

'I've told Jed that I'd joined you up

as an associate member, Isla, just until you officially join us.'

'And that somehow it had slipped his memory; that he hadn't mentioned it to anyone apart from John,' Jed said, raising his eyes skywards.

'For which I apologise,' the older man said, inclining his head. 'The situation has never arisen before, so I've put you in a different category from everyone else, Isla.'

Jed was studying Isla's work and she wondered what he thought, although she didn't really care, she told herself. He was obviously one of those arrogant, self-opinionated types who liked nothing better than to throw his weight around.

'Do you always paint landscapes?' he asked presently.

'No, but I've selected these because they were already mounted and framed. I like all the places I've painted. I've spent several holidays in the Lake District and love the changing colours of the scenery — especially in the autumn.'

'A lady after my own heart. It's one

of my favourite places too, and you've captured it admirably,' Jerome Rowley told her. 'I can really imagine myself walking beside that lake in the autumn.'

Jed didn't comment any further, and presently went off to the back of the workshop to speak with some visitors who were taking a look at John's pottery. He handed out some leaflets about the other venues in the open weekend, and mentioned the summer school, all the while fully aware of the young woman standing beside John Ainsworth, chatting to his father.

When the visitors had moved on, Jed gave a surreptitious glance in Isla's direction. Snatches of the conversation drifted across. He liked the musical lilt in her voice. He thought she was quite pretty with her thick honey-blonde hair and large, rich brown eyes. She had a fresh complexion, a generous mouth and was petite with a nice figure.

Jed acknowledged that Isla Milne had somehow managed to inveigle herself into the art group and make an impression on his father. Her paintings were above the average run-of-the-mill efforts of some aspiring artists. There was something about Isla's work that would make people look and look again.

Jed stooped to recover a couple of leaflets that had spilled onto the floor. He had a strange feeling that Isla Milne was going to make her presence felt in Woodbridge, and not just because of her artwork.

Jerome Rowley signalled to his son that he was ready to leave and, after a few more minutes, the pair of them moved off.

'Oh, well, at least I haven't been given my marching orders,' Isla said, more cheerfully than she felt.

'No — Jerome was very appreciative. You'll be an asset to our group, Isla.'

'Thanks John, I certainly hope so. It looks as though I've got a lot to live up to.'

He consulted the clock. 'Anyway, we're all set and raring to go. My first demonstration's in half an hour.'

'What does Jed Rowley do?' Isla asked, as they waited for some more visitors to appear.

'He's a bronze and clay sculptor. Extremely gifted fellow — takes commissions.'

'Really?' Isla was impressed. 'So, does he do that full time?'

'Oh, no. He works for two or three days a week at some London college, then spends the rest of the time following his own pursuits, which includes keeping tabs on the business side of affairs at Rowley Grange,' John said. At that moment, the door opened, and a group of visitors appeared.

The rest of the morning passed in a flash; Isla was so fascinated by John's demonstrations that she didn't leave the workshop until twelve thirty. To her delight, she had made two sales. John said he was shutting up shop for an hour and going to the pub with some friends. She declined his offer to join them and wandered into the barn, which was an amazing hive of activity.

Several ladies from the spinning guild were in one corner and she went to take a look. They were giving a demonstration, and Isla was fascinated to learn how they dyed the wool using various methods, including placing it in a microwave. The finished results were impressive. They explained that they went to different fairs and attractions in Kent.

She spent a time admiring some of the items on display that they had knitted from the wool: colourful bags, hats and scarfs, beside a variety of decorations.

It was one o'clock already. She decided to have lunch there, as she was needed back at Ivy Cottage by two o'clock.

'Here you are.' She looked up to find Jerome Rowley smiling at her and carrying a loaded tray. 'I saw John outside the *White Hart* just now. He said he thought you'd still be here. Mind if I join you?'

She wondered if he'd changed his mind about the associate membership, after all. Perhaps his son had persuaded him. She wondered where Jed was.

'Jed's gone off to check on his own exhibits.' Jerome Rowley said, just as if he'd been reading her mind. 'I've been walking around rather a lot and felt I deserved a rest. How are your paintings doing?'

'Oh, I've sold a couple and that's two more than I expected,' she told him.

'Nonsense, they're very good. I was impressed with the photographs of your work you emailed to me, and presently I'm going back to the workshop to take another look at those you're exhibiting today. So, you're going to be staying around for a while?'

She nodded, her mouth full of salad baguette.

He drank his coffee. 'How come we've never run into you before? The Ainsworths must have been here for what — three years?'

'Yes, about that. I've been living with

my grandmother and she's been ill for the past eighteen months. She moved into a retirement home recently.'

He nodded and didn't ask any more questions. There were a lot of questions she would have liked to have asked him too, regarding the summer school, but just then the vicar and his wife came across to speak to him. Jerome introduced them as Tim and Penny Pearson, and the conversation reverted to village matters and the weekend's events.

'So, are we likely to see you at church?' Penny asked Isla. 'We've got an early service this week so that anyone who wants to can attend — nine until ten.'

'I'd like to come but I'm not quite sure what's happening tomorrow morning,' Isla told her.

Penny nodded. 'Well if you get the opportunity you must at least take a look round the church. It's very beautiful, but then I'm biased. The stained-glass windows are quite something — medieval and absolutely gorgeous. The tower's open today, if you've a head for heights. The view from the top is amazing.'

It was fast approaching two o'clock so, with a hasty apology, Isla shot off back to Ivy Cottage to find Ellen champing at the bit.

'Isla, have you switched your phone off? I was beginning to think you'd forgotten you were supposed to be here by two o'clock.'

'And here I am, with two minutes to spare and raring to go,' Isla said lightly. 'I was talking to Jerome Rowley and the vicar and his wife. What can I do?'

'Go in the garden and collect the dirty crocks for a start. Amy will be back shortly; her mother's holding the fort at one of the other venues this afternoon and I've promised to look in.'

Once Amy turned up, Isla persuaded her aunt to take a well-deserved break. The afternoon shot by. One of the other artists, Alice, turned up with an older lady, who she referred to as Aunty June, who quickly made herself indispensable by taking charge of the teas, leaving the others to deal with everything else.

There was a steady trickle of visitors wandering appreciatively from room to room. Several of them purchased cards and small items of Jane's jewellery, and an American couple bought two of Ellen's cushions.

It was almost four o'clock when the door opened and Jed Rowley appeared, accompanied by a slim, elegantly dressed woman, beautifully made up with shining ash-blonde hair cut to her shoulders.

'Is Ellen around?' Jed asked.

'Not at the moment. Can I give her a message?' Isla asked.

'Not really — Nicole here is interested in textiles and I've showed her the photos I took on my phone this morning. She's keen to see Ellen's work and wants to speak with her in person . . . Nicole, this is Ellen's niece, Isla Milne, and another of our artists, Amy Bradshaw — Isla, Amy — this is Nicole Trent.'

Nicole gave her a cursory glance. 'I thought the artists would be available to talk about their exhibits.'

'Oh, I'm sure she'll be back shortly,' Amy said. 'She's with my mother at one of the other venues.' She whipped her mobile out of her pocket. 'I'll give her a ring.'

'Her exhibits are in the next room. Would you like me to show you?' Isla led the way into the dining-room where they stood studying Ellen's work.

'I like what I'm seeing,' Nicole said at last, flicking back her hair.' What a pity there isn't any more.'

'Oh, she's sold some already and there wasn't the space to display too much,' Isla told her, wishing Ellen would hurry up.

Hearing voices, Aunty June poked her head round the door, providing a welcome distraction. 'Would anyone like a cup of tea or coffee?'

'Aunty June!' exclaimed Jed. 'How lovely to see you again.' The elderly lady beamed, and he kissed her on the cheek and then, catching her by the arm, drew her into the room.

'Nicole, this lady used to run the village store years back, when we were children. We used to spend our pocket money on the wonderful selection of sweets she sold. I'd love a cup of tea, Aunty June, if you're making one — Nicole?'

'No thanks. We really ought to be making a move, Jed. Don't forget we're dining with the Feltons tonight.'

'So we are. Sorry, Aunty June — perhaps another time.'

To Isla's relief, everyone arrived together shortly after this: Ellen and Jane first, followed by John and Alan.

After the introductions had been made, Nicole said without preamble, 'I'm responsible for organising the soft furnishings in some show homes in the Docklands area. I like what I've seen of your work, Ellen. Would you be prepared to accept a commission?'

Ellen looked frankly stunned. After a moment, she said, 'At any other time

I'd have accepted like a shot, Nicole, but John and I are off to New Zealand shortly and there wouldn't be time. Perhaps on my return I could get in touch.'

'Certainly, but I can't guarantee there'd be an opening.'

Jed had been listening to the conversation and now he looked at John in disbelief. 'Is your forthcoming trip to New Zealand something else my father has neglected to tell me about?'

John looked awkward. 'I suppose you're thinking about the summer school?'

'Too right I am. You can hardly conduct your classes from the other side of the world.'

'This is hardly the time or the place,' Ellen began, but they ignored her.

'There really isn't a problem,' John assured him in his reasonable manner. 'I'm around for the first two courses and then, after that, Sam is going to step in. Isla will be there too, to assist.'

Jed Rowley's green eyes glinted.

'That's what you think, is it? We'll have to see about that. I'm surprised at you, John — I really am. Come on Nicole, We've got a dinner party to go to,' and taking her by the arm, he steered her out of the room.

There was an uncomfortable silence, only broken by Aunty June bustling in once more to enquire, 'Tea or coffee anyone?'

Fortunately, some late visitors turned up at that point and, after a few more minutes, Isla and Amy felt they could leave Ivy Cottage and go off to take a quick look at some of the other venues.

3

'Jed wasn't too pleased, was he?' Amy commented, as they set off in the direction of one of the other workshops.

'No, John has dropped me in it good and proper. Ellen only told me yesterday about their New Zealand trip and I really don't have a clue what's happening regarding the summer school. I'd understood I was supposed to be taking some painting classes and that it had all been arranged. Nothing's been said about assisting with any pottery classes. I sent stuff off by e-mail a couple of months back to someone called Dominic Irwin.'

'Mm, that's Jerome Rowley's administrator and general organiser. Actually, he also happens to be my boyfriend Dale's brother.'

'Really! Is everyone related to everyone else round here?'

Amy grinned. 'Not quite ... So,

didn't you have to come for an interview?

Isla shook her head. 'No — just a fairly informal Skype call with Jerome Rowley. John vouched for me, and the college where I used to work provided references. John has lots of useful contacts. The problem is there hasn't been time for a proper discussion with him since I've been here, and this has come as a bit of a bombshell.'

Amy shrugged. 'Oh, I shouldn't worry about it, if I were you. There's obviously been some sort of breakdown in communication. It'll get sorted.'

Isla thought of Jed Rowley's expression and hoped Amy was right. Isla seemed to have been inveigled into a situation that wasn't of her own making.

'What do you make of Nicole?' Amy asked now.

'I — um — she seemed pleasant enough. Very elegant. Is she his fiancée?'

Amy shook her head. 'She's new on

47

the scene. Haven't seen her in Woodbridge before. Probably someone he's met through work. I bet her clothes weren't bought from any high street store.'

Isla thought fleetingly of Nicole and decided that she was probably a good match for Jed Rowley. Both obviously liked throwing their weight around. But then she remembered how he'd softened at the sight of Aunty June. He obviously had a different side. She was surprised that he was still living at home, but then recalled that his father had been ill. Perhaps he had returned to the Grange to be nearer to him.

'Jed is very good looking — don't you think?' Amy asked.

'I suppose so,' Isla conceded grudgingly, remembering his lean features, slightly long, wavy fair hair and those expressive sea-green eyes. 'So, are we going to look at your work now, Amy?'

'If you like. No — come to think of it, they'll be packing up for the day now. Why don't we leave it until tomorrow? A lot of mine is in the garden and the sun's gone in.' She consulted the booklet in her hand. 'Tell you what — let's go to Laburnam Cottage, where Jed's work is on display.'

Despite herself, Isla was keen to see Jed's work, and at least he wouldn't be around.

★ ★ ★

Laburnum Cottage was delightful. Isla would like to have lingered in the garden, but there wasn't time for her to have more than a glimpse of the old English roses, hollyhocks and red brick paths. Inside she was introduced to the Franklin family, who owned the cottage, and spent a few minutes chatting to them before having a look around.

Jed's sculptures were in the back room and she could see that he was extremely talented. It was as if he had breathed life into his bronze figures and animals. She stood transfixed.

'Great, aren't they?' Amy commented.

'Such detail and skill. I'd buy one myself, but I can't afford his prices.'

Isla gasped as she spotted one of the price tags. 'Do people really pay that sort of money?'

'It would seem so. He's made quite a name for himself so folk are prepared to pay top prices as a form of investment. He accepts commissions, too.'

'Yes, John said.' Isla recognised Jed Rowley's talent and suddenly understood why he would only be prepared to accept the highest standard from others. She realised he had set the bar high and hoped she could meet his expectations.

They were just about to leave Laburnham Cottage when they heard voices, and a moment later Jane Bradshaw came into the room with a tall, dark-haired young man.

'Oh, good. I thought this was where you'd most likely be. Isla, this is Dominic Irwin, Jerome Rowley's administrator. Dom, this is Isla Milne.'

They exchanged greetings. Isla's first impression of Dominic Irwin was that he was very pleasant but rather serious.

Shortly afterwards, Isla and Amy left the cottage. As they were walking back along the road, Amy yawned prodigiously. 'It's been a long day. Dale and I were going clubbing tonight, but I need to conserve my energy for tomorrow, so we'll probably just go out for a meal instead. What about you?'

'Oh, a long soak in the bath and an early night, I expect,' Isla said. 'It's been a pretty full-on couple of days — weeks, actually.'

Amy darted a look at her. 'So, is there anyone special in your life?'

'Apart from my Gran, you mean?' Isla asked.

Amy chuckled. 'Tell me to mind my own business if you like.'

Isla sighed. 'Oh, it's no secret. Up until a year ago there was someone in my life, but when I had to give up work in order to look after Gran, he wasn't as supportive as I'd expected — he couldn't understand why I wasn't prepared to leave her alone in the house to go out with him. In the end we decided to break up. It was a difficult decision at the time, but mutual — it probably saved a lot of heartache at a later date. Ewan wasn't the guy I thought he was, so if I'd married him, it could have only ended in divorce.'

'Tough. So why don't you join us tonight? There's a nice pub near where we live that serves good food. Dale could ask one of his mates to make a foursome.'

'No, thanks — I'm not looking for another relationship,' Isla said, more sharply than she intended. Seeing Amy's surprised expression, she added, 'But thanks anyway — perhaps another time.'

'OK, it was just a thought. Anyway, it's been a long day. I'll see you tomorrow.' With a quick wave, Amy turned into a side road.

Isla bit her lip; Amy was a likeable young woman and she hoped she hadn't lost the opportunity of making friends with her. It was just that she needed to take things slowly at the moment; she wasn't into casual relationships. She had decided that if and when she met Mr Right, it would be for ever.

★   ★   ★

Isla was standing in the sunshine amongst the ancient gravestones in the churchyard the following day. She and John had been to the morning service, which had been short but very pleasant. Afterwards, the vicar's wife, Penny, had pounced on her, saying how delighted she was to see her there and introducing her to several members of the congregation. Now Isla was waiting for John, who was engaged in conversation with yet another member of the Art Society.

Suddenly she saw Jed Rowley coming towards her along the path, and she wished John would hurry up. She didn't fancy another confrontation. She dodged round the back of a massive family vault and stooped to read the inscription. She might have known it: it was the Rowleys'.

'We've got a lot of ancestors,' a voice said beside her. Startled, she shot up, stubbing her toe on the sharp edge of the vault. It was excruciatingly painful, and she yelled out. Jed's arm caught hers.

'Lean on me — there's a bench just over there.'

She sank down thankfully. Blood streaked her toe, and she felt a complete fool.

'Are you OK or do you want a lift home?'

She shook her head. 'I'm fine, thanks,' she said, taking a grip of herself. 'You startled me.'

'Sorry — I seem to make a habit of doing that, but hopefully I'm not really that scary,' he told her with a wry smile.

The arm resting on hers was comforting, and just for a moment, she was filled with a sudden and inexplicable emotion. Her pulse began to race.

'Isla, we really need to talk,' he said, without further preamble.

'Yes, of course, but not today,' she told him coolly, regaining her composure.

His green eyes glinted. 'OK, but it needs to be soon. There are things to discuss. I'm in London tomorrow and Tuesday, so how about Wednesday?'

Isla nodded. Her eyes fixed on John, who was coming out of the church deep in conversation with Jed's father.

'Come up to the Grange for coffee around eleven.' Before she could reply, Jed had left her side and caught up with his father. She watched the pair of them walk off in the direction of the lychgate.

Staring after Jed Rowley, she realised that her immediate future in Woodbridge was in his hands; the thought was disturbing.

'Oh, it'll just be a formality. Jed likes to have everything cut and dried,' John said when she told him. 'Anyway, I can run through a few things with you beforehand.'

'I'm a bit mystified, John. I under-stood I was just engaged to take a couple of painting courses at the summer school at Rowley Grange, but now it seems I'm assisting this Sam with your pottery course whilst you're in New Zealand.'

John rubbed his chin. 'Yes, about that — you see, I booked the holiday recently. We originally decided we'd have to postpone it, but then when the house sale went through, I rang my brother to see if the invitation was still open. By then my last pottery course was fully booked and I couldn't face disappointing all those students.'

'So you roped in your friend and assumed I'd help out too?'

John looked awkward. 'Everything happened in a heap. I was hoping to get to talk to you before now, but yesterday was manic and . . . '

She grinned at his contrite expres-sion. 'It's OK, John, I get the picture. I'd love to help out although, as you know, pottery has never been my strength.'

'But you understand the basics and that's the most important thing. The people who signed up for the first course are more or less beginners just wanting to try their hand at something different. The rest are students from my other classes who already know the ropes and want more practice or just time to finish their projects.'

'Well, if you put it like that, how can I refuse? Now all I have to do is convince Jed Rowley that I'm not completely incompetent.'

★   ★   ★

The open day was similar to the previous one, but more relaxed. Isla began to enjoy herself and after lunch John encouraged her to take some time out. Ellen had enough helpers that afternoon.

She caught up with Amy at Gardenia House, who was standing beside a young man dressed in uniform jeans and white T-shirt; a small girl was sitting on a window seat.

'Dale, my boyfriend, and my niece, Skye. She's seven and an absolute character. I'm keeping an eye on her while my sister's having a wander round.'

'Hi,' Isla said, shaking Dale's hand and waving at Skye. The little girl came dancing across, holding aloft a carefully coloured picture.

'Someone had the bright idea of printing off some cards for the children to colour in.' Amy explained. 'We originally thought about beaded friendship-bracelets, but we have to be a bit careful where little ones are concerned.'

'Mm — beads up noses, et cetera. That's lovely, Skye, and I do like your name. I've never met anyone called Skye before.'

The small girl beamed at Isla. 'Guess what it means.' Isla shook her head.

'Sky — that's what it means!' The little girl giggled and pointed to the blue sky on her picture.

'Well, I never would have guessed that! So, where's your work, Amy?'

'Over here.' She led the way across the room to a display cabinet, its contents illuminated. Isla stared, transfixed at the delicate glass vases and jewellery.

'Wow! Those are gorgeous — so individual.'

'There are some fun things around the garden too — garden glass. Come and see,' Amy invited.

'Can I come too?' Skye asked.

'OK, but you've seen them lots of times already, poppet.'

They made their way into the cottage garden, which was breathtakingly beautiful and a wonderful setting for the glass decorations and dreamcatchers hanging from the trees and placed on metal spikes in large ceramic pots on the patio.

'This is my very favourite one,' Skye told Isla, pointing to a brightly coloured parrot suspended from a Rowan tree. 'Which one is yours?'

'I like them all but perhaps that one the most,' Isla told the little girl, as she stopped to examine a large glass sunflower in tones of gold and brown. 'You are clever, Amy.'

Amy looked pleased. 'Oh, I don't know about that — I just enjoy making them. I'm never quite sure how they're going to turn out and that's part of the fun.'

'Have you sold many?'

'A few, but the folk who bought them have arranged to collect them later. To my amazement I've had one or two orders too.'

Skye had raced ahead to the bottom of the garden where, over the fence, Isla could see a couple of donkeys contentedly sunning themselves in a field.

'Skye's in her element here. She lives in the town. She's arty too, unlike my sister who isn't the slightest bit interested, but always comes to support these events. To be fair she's very musical and I'm not.'

They sat on a rustic bench for a few minutes. Looking around her at the peaceful scene, Isla realised she could find inspiration to paint here.

'Did you have a good time at the pub last night?'

'We didn't get there after all. In the end we settled for a Chinese takeaway and curled up on the sofa and watched a box set.'

'Just as well I didn't accept your invitation to join you then.'

Amy grinned. 'Oh, there'll be other occasions and next time I won't take no for an answer, but I promise I won't try and match-make.'

★   ★   ★

The day finally drew to a close and, after they had eaten, and Isla had helped Ellen tidy up, she phoned her grandmother. It felt as if she had been at Ivy Cottage for weeks instead of a couple of days.

'I'm absolutely fine, dear, so there's no need to worry about me,' Martha Milne told her granddaughter. 'Presently, I'm joining some of my new friends for a game of cards. Tell me about your weekend. It sounded as if it was going to be very interesting.'

Isla gave her grandmother an edited account.

'I'm glad it went well for you. Now, I wouldn't mind a few words with Ellen before I go, if you could get her for me.'

The few words seemed to turn into quite a lengthy discussion, as Isla realised Ellen was telling her mother about their forthcoming trip to New Zealand. Isla went into the sitting-room and picked up a magazine. When Ellen finally came off the phone, she said with slightly heightened colour, 'I don't know what you said to your grand-mother, Isla, but she seems to be under the impression that we're taking advantage of you by expecting you to hold the fort here whilst we're in New Zealand.'

Isla swallowed. 'I haven't mentioned New Zealand to Gran, Ellen.'

John looked up from his paper. 'I'm afraid that was me, Ellen. I thought it was about time one of us said something — let her get used to the idea.'

Ellen pursed her lips. 'Yes, well, it's not as if we're going tomorrow, as I told her. Now, is someone going to help me take my exhibition stuff upstairs?'

★   ★   ★

Isla had wondered how Ellen was filling her days now she'd given up work. She soon realised that her aunt had a wide circle of friends who met up for coffee mornings and lunches. She was on several committees and belonged to various groups. Isla contented herself in the garden. It had been a long time since she'd been able to relax.

'I'm going shopping in London tomorrow — fancy coming with me?' Ellen asked on Tuesday afternoon.

'I'd love to, Ellen, but I've got a meeting with Jed Rowley at eleven o'clock, if you remember. I assume it's about the summer school, so I don't want to cancel.'

'Oh, well, thought I'd ask. I'm meeting up with a friend of mine for lunch, so you'd probably have been bored anyway.'

The thought of a day's shopping in London would have appealed to Isla, but it couldn't be helped. It was no use putting off the meeting with Jed Rowley, even though she was feeling apprehensive.

4

On Wednesday morning Isla deliberated about what to wear for her meeting with Jed Rowley. In the end, she settled for a pair of smart navy trousers and an attractive multi-coloured blouse. She twisted her honey-blonde hair into a top knot.

It was a fine June day and so she decided to walk to Rowley Grange. Reaching the gate she'd passed several times before, she set off along the tree-lined drive but soon realised she hadn't taken into account how long it was. It was almost ten past eleven when she rang the doorbell.

The door flew open and Jed Rowley said abruptly, 'I was beginning to think you'd forgotten.'

It was not a good start, but she refused to let him intimidate her. 'Good morning, Mr Rowley. I apologise for being a few minutes late. I set off in good time, but I've walked, and it took longer than I expected.'

His expression changed. 'Right. Well, I approve of your consideration for the carbon footprint but remind me to show you the short cut. Come along in. My father's playing golf this morning, but he has made a few notes and sends his apologies for not being here.'

He showed her into a large, book-lined room which obviously served as a study as well as a library. She sat on the chair he indicated, opposite a huge mahogany partner's desk. There was a tray of coffee on a side table, and she wondered if he'd made it or if he had someone to do it for him.

The upkeep of the house must be enormous, she decided. He handed her the coffee and then passed a plate of shortbread biscuits.

'How's the toe?' he enquired unexpectedly.

'Better, thanks, or I wouldn't have walked.'

'Obviously.' He leant back in his chair, crossing his legs, and surveyed her, taking in her slender figure, attractive features and pretty hair. 'So, what did you think of our open weekend?'

'I thoroughly enjoyed it,' Isla told him honestly. 'There was such an amazing variety of exhibits on display — so much talent. I have to admit though: I was a bit confused trying to sort out who was who.'

Jed smiled. 'Yes, it can be a bit daunting at first, but they're a friendly crowd. Now, to get down to business. I've spoken with John on the phone and he assures me that you're sufficiently qualified to assist with his final course.'

'Yes, about that . . . ' Isla began, but he waved his hand impatiently.

'If you would just hear me out. I'll be absolutely honest: I expressed a few doubts. I'm not at all pleased that he's rescinded on his agreement to take all three courses. John was running courses here way before he moved into the area, and his reputation goes before him.'

She nodded. 'I appreciate you would prefer someone more experienced. John has rather dropped me in it.'

He sighed and drank some of his coffee. 'Oh, well. I suppose beggars can't be choosers.'

She gasped and glared at him. 'Thank you very much for your vote of confidence! For your information I knew nothing about helping out with John's pottery course. I'd understood I was engaged to take two painting courses only, but then I didn't know about the trip to New Zealand until Friday afternoon either!'

His eyes widened in incredulity. 'Are you telling me that John just took it for granted that you'd step in and help him out of a hole?'

She nodded. 'John is a dear man but sometimes he can be quite exasperating. I was interviewed by your father on a Skype call for the painting courses, but I can assure you nothing was said about pottery. I quite understand if you'd prefer to find someone else to do that — although I was hoping to carry on with the painting courses.'

He entwined his fingers and sat in silence for a few minutes, giving her the opportunity to study him. She decided he had to be in his mid-thirties. His thick fair hair was expertly cut; he had a prominent forehead and a strong, determined jaw line. His eyes were the colour of the sea.

'Let's go back to the pottery for a moment or two. I admit I do have some reservations. I would need to see an outline of what you propose to do.'

'That's straightforward enough. John and I had a discussion last night. I'm just proposing to follow on with his plan. He's got oceans of notes and talked me through it briefly, but we'll obviously do so in more depth before he leaves. Also, I'd like to sit in on one or two of his sessions, because I realise our approach might be slightly different. Obviously, time's too short during these courses to do more than skim the surface and give the students a taster.'

He nodded. 'There is something else. Perhaps John has already said — Sam, who assists John on these occasions, and is a good friend of his, only works part-time because his wife is disabled. He's a brilliant potter and wonderful character but sometimes needs to leave early; which is why he can't be totally in charge of the course. He's a bit sensitive about it, but I suspect he doesn't have an easy home life.'

This was something else that John had neglected to tell her. 'That's fine — absolutely no problem. I've been used to helping my grandmother who has mobility problems, so understand the situations that can arise.'

He nodded. 'Oh, of course. John mentioned Ellen's mother had gone into a home recently and that's why you'd be living with them.'

'It's only a temporary measure,' Isla assured him. 'Anyway, perhaps you ought to be speaking with this Sam and asking how he'd feel about working with me.'

His green eyes glinted, and she noted the little laughter lines in the corners. 'I already have, as a matter of fact. He doesn't have any issues — says he's looking forward to meeting you. John's already sounded him out, apparently. He just neglected to do the same with us.'

Isla gave a little smile. 'Typical John! Hopefully that's settled then. So, what about my painting courses? Your father and Dominic Irwin didn't have a problem and as far as I'm aware, I've been booked for those two weeks.'

'Yes, I realise that now. I was on a trip to Italy with a group of students at that time, and somehow hadn't managed to catch up with everything that was going on around here. Anyway, I've seen samples of your work and can see that you've got ability. Dominic showed me the course plan that you'd e-mailed him. It's very professional.'

'Then hopefully I've managed to convince you that I'm capable of running both courses?'

His expression was unfathomable. 'Yes, well, we'll just have to see how it works out, won't we? I'll leave it to John to give you the conducted tour of the building where you'll be working.'

'But I thought — I mean, isn't it here?' she asked, puzzled.

'Good gracious, no. My father wouldn't allow that. It's situated in the Arts Centre, which is conveniently near to the workshops and barn. It would be a good idea if you could familiarise yourself with your workspace beforehand. There are a number of things you'll need to know, such as catering arrangements. Students of every age always seem to be interested in their meal breaks! Anyway, all will be revealed shortly . . . Now, can I offer you more coffee?'

'No, thanks.' She placed her cup and saucer on the tray.

'Do you have any further questions?'

'Not for the moment. I've got a much clearer idea of what's expected of me.' She had no intention of admitting that she was feeling slightly overwhelmed.

He got to his feet. 'Good — then how about I show you that short cut? I could do with a breath of fresh air.'

Jed ushered Isla to the door, and his fingers brushed against her as he opened it for her. His touch set her pulse racing and she caught her breath at the unexpectedness of it. Almost against her will, she had to admit that he was very attractive.

They set off through a small wooded area to the side of the Grange.

'In the spring, there are clusters of primroses here and, shortly afterwards, it's ablaze with bluebells and patches of wild garlic. It's a real painter's paradise.'

'It sounds delightful.' Her smile spoke of genuine delight, he decided.

'So, have you always lived in Woodbridge?' she asked curiously.

'Practically. We moved here when I was around fourteen when my grandfather died. My father, as the eldest son, inherited the estate.'

'Isn't it unusual to have both a manor and a grange in such close proximity?' she wanted to know.

'Not at all. There are several places I could name where that's happened. Sometimes they're owned by members of the same family.'

He paused to open a small, wrought iron gate, and she followed him along a narrow track by the side of a field where sheep grazed peacefully.

'What about you, Isla? Did you always live in Sussex?'

'Most of my life, although I was actually born in Kent, not far from here. We moved to Bexhill-on-Sea when I was very small. We lived with my grandparents, but my mother died when I was twelve.'

'Ellen's sister?' Jed asked.

'Yes. My grandparents brought me up after that.'

'Which is why you wanted to look after your grandmother?'

Isla nodded. 'Yes. She's been very good to me.'

Fortunately, they had reached the end of the track which came out near the church and workshops. She hoped he wouldn't ask her about her father, but perhaps John had filled him in with that too. She knew Ellen wouldn't divulge anything; not that there was too much to divulge. One day, perhaps Isla might attempt to track down the father who wasn't named on her birth certificate. Isla often thought Gran and Ellen knew more than they were prepared to say.

Jed turned to look at her. 'Right. You know your way from here. I felt that was quite a productive meeting. We've covered a lot of ground this morning.' He put out his hand, and as she shook it, she was sharply aware of the contact of his fingers with hers and it was all she could do not to react. It was as if there was a kind of magnetism emanating from him.

★   ★   ★

At breakfast on Saturday, Isla announced her intention of visiting her grandmother.

Ellen frowned. 'But you've only been here five minutes, Isla. Why don't you leave it a while longer? After all, my mother needs to get used to the fact that you're not just living a stone's throw away anymore.'

'Yes, but I don't want her thinking I've forgotten her, so I'd rather go now whilst I've got the opportunity,' Isla told her, surprised at her aunt's attitude.

'I'll come with you,' John offered, 'and then I can explain a bit more about our trip to New Zealand. So how about you, Ellen — are you going to join us?'

Ellen screwed a lid on tightly to a jar of honey, her body language speaking volumes. 'I've told you what I think, but you must please yourself. Anyway, I'm meeting up with Jane and some of the others this morning to discuss the next open weekend.'

She was tight-lipped, and there was an uncomfortable silence during which Isla cleared away the breakfast things, wondering what the problem was.

Shortly afterwards, John and Isla set off for Bexhill. 'I'm picking up vibes. Is there a problem between Gran and my aunt — other than the New Zealand trip?'

John paused, 'Oh, nothing you need worry your head about. There *was* something a few years back, but it's history and nothing can be done about it now, so we just have to move on. One day, when the time is right, I'm sure either Gran or Ellen will tell you.'

'Does that mean it concerns me?' Isla asked, her curiosity aroused.

'Look, my lips are sealed — it's more than my life's worth to say any more,' John told her cryptically. Isla wished he hadn't said anything at all, rather than leaving things hanging in mid-air. Her imagination worked overtime as she racked her brain for anything that might have caused tension regarding herself. Perhaps Ellen had been against her living at Ivy Cottage. She had certainly not shown any encouragement regarding her participation in the open weekends.

When they arrived at the home, they were shown into the conservatory, where Martha Milne was chatting to one of the other residents. She was a smartly dressed lady in her mid-eighties, her short silver hair beautifully styled. She looked delighted to see them but peered over John's shoulder, a slight frown on her brow.

'So, where's Ellen?'

'Oh, I'm afraid she was unavoidably detained, Martha. Had a prior engagement that she couldn't get out of. As Isla was coming, I said I'd join her.'

'I see. Well, it's good of the pair of you to spare the time,' she said, rather huffily.

A member of staff arrived pushing a drinks trolley, and the awkward moment passed as they helped to hand round the teas and coffees to those sitting nearby.

'Gran, you do like being here, don't you?' Isla asked, uncomfortably aware of a slightly strained atmosphere. There was something she couldn't put her finger on.

'Yes, it's very comfortable and the staff are lovely. I couldn't wish for better care. Of course, I miss my home, but you've all got your own lives to lead and I'm determined not to be selfish. Anyway, enough of that — tell me about this New Zealand trip, John. That's come as a bolt out of the blue.'

'Not really Martha. My brother Graham invited us to his daughter's wedding quite a while ago and we originally declined. But now that you're settled here and the house sale has gone through, we felt we could accept, after all.'

Gran looked at Isla. 'And what about you, love? I had hoped you'd be going on holiday, now that you don't have me to worry about. Thought you might even get back with Ewan.'

Isla took her grandmother's hand and said gently, 'That's not going to happen, Gran. As for going on holiday — well, I shall enjoy being in

Woodbridge. It's a complete change of scenery and I'm looking forward to the summer school, so please don't give it another thought.'

Martha patted her granddaughter's hand. 'I don't know how I'd have managed without you these past months, but now you deserve a proper break. What do you think, John?'

John shifted uncomfortably on his chair. 'I obviously agree with you, Martha. Perhaps Isla will feel more like going away by the time we get back.'

'And when's that likely to be? You didn't actually say.'

John stirred his coffee vigorously. 'That's because we're not 100% sure. It's all a bit last-minute and we're still finalising our plans.'

Martha helped herself to a bourbon biscuit. 'And when do you set off on this trip?'

'Let's see. At the beginning of August. My niece gets married during the second week.'

John elaborated a bit more on their

holiday plans, but Isla got the impression that her grandmother was only half listening.

'I thought you were taking courses at Rowley Grange when college finished, like you usually do.'

'Yes, I am. At least, I'm taking the first two, and half of the third.'

'I'm covering for John's last course at Rowley Grange,' Isla told her.

'As well as taking those painting classes?'

'It's no problem, Gran. I'm looking forward to it.'

Martha Milne looked unconvinced. 'Hmm — didn't you say Sam Westfield was working with you, John? Can't he take the course?'

'He and Isla will be taking it between them.'

Gran's eyebrows arched. 'Is that so! Well, I only hope you know what you're doing.'

She shot John a meaningful glance, and Isla wondered what it was about. The name Westfield rang a bell, but she couldn't for the life of her think why. There was obviously something going on here that she didn't understand, and it was clear that her family weren't prepared to enlighten her.

'Would you like us to take you out to lunch?' John asked the old lady now.

'No thank you, dear. It's shepherd's pie here today and I always enjoy that. Besides, my friend Dora needs me to help her with some knitting. She's got in a muddle with the pattern. It's a pity you didn't let me know you were coming. You could have had lunch here, but the catering staff prefer to know in advance.'

'Oh well, there'll be another time. We'll be in to see you again soon and next time I'll bring Ellen.'

'Yes, well mind that you do . . . Isla, can you take this bag of goodies you've brought me along to my room? I'll look forward to unpacking it later. Oh, and fetch me my library book would you, love? I think it's on my bedside table. It's a rather gory thriller with a lurid cover in orange and mauve. You can't miss it!'

Isla picked up the carrier bag and took it along to her grandmother's room. She searched in vain for the library book before realising that Gran had probably wanted an excuse to speak with John alone. She wondered what about. Perhaps it was some financial thing, but she dismissed that as unlikely in a room full of people.

As she approached the conservatory, she saw that Gran was indeed deep in conversation with John, confirming her suspicions.

Martha looked up as she approached and waved her library book at her. 'Sorry, love, I sent you on a wild goose chase. It was down the side of my chair all the time!'

'Well, that explains why I couldn't find it,' Isla said lightly, and Gran chuckled.

They didn't stay too much longer after that.

'I fancy fish and chips,' John said as

they drove away from the home. 'What about you?'

'Good idea. I know the very place. They serve mushy peas too.'

'Even better! You're in charge of directions!'

★ ★ ★

'How did you think Gran seemed?' Isla asked presently, as they sat in a little cafe enjoying their fish lunch.

John reached for the tomato ketchup and helped himself liberally, and Isla suppressed a smile, knowing that Ellen wouldn't keep that in the house either. He speared a chip.

'I think she's settled remarkably well in the circumstances. A pity she didn't want to come out for lunch, but I don't expect she wants her routine disrupted.'

Isla nodded. 'Gran's always been a stickler for routine. Aunt Ellen takes after her . . . John, when you mentioned your colleague, Sam, I got the distinct feeling Gran knew him.'

John paused fractionally. 'Oh, I expect she's met him over the years. I've known him for — oh, I don't know how long.'

'Jed Rowley told me Sam's wife is disabled.'

A shadow crossed John's face. 'Yes, she's got severe arthritis. She depends on Sam a lot, but they both make light of it. You'll like him, Isla. Everyone does. Now there's an exhibition I'm keen to see at the De la Warr Pavilion. A pity your friends are out, or we could have dropped in on them.'

It was apparent that John wasn't prepared to tell Isla any more about Sam Westfield. She was just going to have to be patient.

Presently, they had a brisk walk by the sea, which was a deep turquoise that day. The beach was shingle and harsh on the feet, but Isla was used to it and didn't mind. She took in great gulps of bracing sea air, suddenly feeling homesick.

'Are you missing this place?' John

asked, taking her arm.

'I miss the sea and Gran, but I'm enjoying being in Woodbridge. I hadn't realised it was so near to where I'd spent the first few months of my life. I've never really known much about my roots and, to be honest, haven't wanted to until just recently. I must get Gran to tell me a bit about the house where I lived when I was first born.'

A strange look flitted across John's face. 'I'd go easy on that, if I were you, Isla,' he advised.

'Why?' she asked in astonishment. 'I would have thought she'd have been only too happy to talk about it. Would it be better if I spoke to Ellen?'

'No!' he said emphatically, and she shot him a surprised look. There was something going on here that she didn't understand.

'OK,' she said. 'Shall we go and take a look at that art exhibition you were keen to see in the Del la Warr Pavilion?'

'Great.' John looked relieved that Isla wasn't going to pursue the subject, but she decided she was only going to put it on hold for the time being. There were things she needed to know about her parents, and she was determined to find out.

5

A few days later, Isla bumped into Jed Rowley as she was walking back to Ivy Cottage from the workshop where she had been sorting through some of her paintings and sketches. He fell into step beside her.

'I'm just on my way to the meeting at Jane's house regarding this weekend's open studio — is that where you're heading?'

'Actually, no. I haven't been invited.'

Jed frowned. 'Well, I'm inviting you now. It's important as many people as possible are there tonight.'

'But I'm only an associate member,' she reminded him, tongue in cheek, and he shot her a look and then grinned.

'OK, I deserved that. I'll admit I had my reservations, but you've proved your worth. You've certainly impressed my father. He tells me he's bought one of your paintings.'

'Really? John told me I'd sold another one but was vague when I asked him who the purchaser was.'

'So, now you know. That reminds me, I need to see the pair of you soon to finalise some course details.'

She nodded. 'That could be tricky. John's a bit difficult to pin down at the moment. The end of term's fast approaching and he's working flat out at the college to get everything finished. Can I give him a message?'

'Oh, it'll keep. Just as long as we get all the ends tied up before he begins his course. After all, it isn't as if he hasn't done it all before. Quite apart from that. I'd like you to meet Sam — we'll have to arrange something soon.'

'Yes, that would make sense. I'm looking forward to meeting up with him. I've been looking through John's notes and making a few of my own. I'll be interested to see the workspace for my painting group at some point too.'

'As soon as this weekend is out of the way, we'll sort something out,' he promised.

'What time does this meeting start?' Isla asked, conscious of her casual attire.

He consulted his watch. 'As of five minutes ago. I had a phone call on the landline just as I was about to leave.'

'I really ought to tidy up . . . ' she began, as they approached Ivy Cottage.

He surveyed her, his green eyes roving over her slowly so that she coloured beneath his gaze 'Isla, you're an artist; jeans and t-shirts are artists' uniform.'

It was her turn to look at him. He was impeccably dressed in a dark suit with a white shirt and green tie. She wondered if he had a date with Nicole later that evening. The thought filled her with unexpected disquiet.

'You're an artist too,' she pointed out, 'so, shouldn't you be taking a leaf out of your own book?'

He chuckled. 'Of course, but I've just come from a rather different sort of meeting in London.'

She was immediately contrite and ashamed of herself for jumping to conclusions. 'Have you eaten?'

'I grabbed a sandwich and coffee to have on the train. In case you're thinking that's hardly enough for a strapping chap like me, Jane always provides excellent refreshments.'

A few minutes later, they arrived at Jane's house and were ushered into the sitting-room. 'Look who I found in the lane,' Jed said. 'Most of you will have met Ellen's niece, Isla Milne, already. I've encouraged her to join us tonight, as she'll be living in the area for the foreseeable future and helping out with the summer school at Rowley Grange.'

All eyes were focussed on Isla and she could see that Ellen was looking disapproving. Well, it wasn't her fault that Jed had insisted she came in such a high-handed manner, and not given her time to tidy up, Isla thought crossly.

'Budge up,' Alan instructed Amy, and Isla squeezed into the space beside her on the large, squashy sofa. She accepted a glass of wine and did not look in Ellen's direction again.

'You've won him over, then,' Amy whispered.

'Who?' Isla asked, her eyes widening innocently.

Amy grinned. 'Stop pretending. I'm a teacher, remember, so nothing much gets past me. That good-looking hunk over there — who else?'

'Oh, him! He's a bit of a control freak in my opinion. He practically frog-marched me here. I didn't have any choice in the matter!'

Amy's smile widened. 'Well, I for one am glad you came. We could do with some fresh input from younger members.'

Jane and another representative from the WI took the first part of the meeting, which was concerned with general housekeeping matters, mainly to do with the barn. After that, Jed Rowley shuffled the papers in his hand and leant forward in his chair.

'Now the main reason I've asked you here tonight is because, as some of you will already know, the Franklins have had a family crisis — which is why they're unable to be here this evening *and* can't be around this weekend. As you're aware, several members of their family contribute at Laburnum Cottage, together with me and Sandra. She can't be around either, due to a conference she can't get out of — although we knew that already. The Franklins have kindly agreed to us going ahead and using the venue, providing I'm overall responsible for it.

'I'm sure you'll appreciate that I can't be around all the time, as I need to be available at the other places, so I'll need some volunteers or it can't stay open.'

Amy nudged Isla and she nodded. 'We will,' they said, practically in unison.

'How would that fit in with everyone else?' Jed enquired.

'Oh, we'll manage,' Ellen said, rather grudgingly.

'If John takes care of his workshop then I can still be available to help you out for an hour or so,' Isla promised her.

'And the second weekend's always easier,' Jane said positively.

'Well, that's settled, thanks to Amy and Isla. I'll email both of you some info about the work on display at Laburnum Cottage once I've got back to the Franklins.'

Shortly afterwards, they drew up a rota and the meeting broke up. Isla realised she was beginning to feel more integrated in Woodbridge and, in a strange sort of way, that it was down to Jed Rowley.

★ ★ ★

Ellen's mood considerably improved the following day when she received a large bouquet of flowers from Nicole. It was in appreciation for Ellen putting her in touch with one of her textile and design friends, Christina, who was on a similar wavelength to Ellen.

'It's good to be appreciated,' Ellen said, sniffing the flowers. 'Christina will do a sterling job; although I have to admit I'd have liked to have been in a position to have accepted that commission myself. Opportunities like that don't come along very often,' she added wistfully.

Isla stared at Ellen in surprise. 'But you do want to go to New Zealand?'

'Absolutely. I wasn't able to accompany John before, when he went to his cousin's funeral, so there's no way I'd let him down for a second time. It's just that the timing could have been better.'

Isla felt a tinge of sympathy for her aunt. She had always thought Ellen had it all, but now she was beginning to see things rather differently.

As she helped Ellen arrange the flowers, she said, 'Perhaps you'll get some inspiration whilst you're away. You could create a website to sell your stuff like John. You are very talented, Ellen.'

'Thanks for that, Isla. You're no mean

artist yourself. It would appear to run in the family. Your grandfather was a good artist, and your mother too.'

Ellen rarely mentioned Isla's mother, Leona. Martha Milne had kept the memories alive for her granddaughter by putting a number of things into a box, but there was no artwork apart from a small sketch of herself as a little girl.

'I wish I knew a bit more about her. It's only recently that I've realised you all lived near Woodbridge at one time. Was that why you chose to move here?'

Ellen tweaked one or two flowers into place before replying.

'John wanted to come here for a number of reasons. It wouldn't have been my first choice, but there has to be a certain amount of give and take in a marriage. He knew this area well, because he was already involved with the Art Society and the summer school.'

'And, of course, you were still working for the first year or so after you came here.'

'Yes.' Ellen stood back to admire the

flower arrangement. 'Actually, it's turning out better than I'd expected. I'm making new friends and John's in his element so what's not to like! And what about you, Isla? Do you think you're going to like living here?'

'Actually, I think I am.' Isla said, and realised that she meant it.

'Is there any chance you might get back with Ewan?'

'No way!' she told her aunt, more forcibly than she intended. 'Sorry, but I've already had this conversation with Gran. Ewan and I are history. We just weren't compatible.'

'Then it's as well you found out before you decided to get married. You've got a sensible head on your shoulders — unlike me when I was younger.'

Isla stared at her in surprise. 'But you and John . . . ?'

'Oh, I don't mean John. I got married for the first time when I was just turned twenty-two, believing that love was all that mattered in a relationship.'

'Yes, of course. I tend to forget

you've been married before, because it seems like you've been married to John for ever.'

'Eighteen years this year. I was only married to Tom for ten before we divorced . . . I don't suppose you remember him?'

'Well, yes, I do actually. Not clearly, of course, because I was only a little girl. He was always kind to me. You were at Art College with him, weren't you?'

'Yes. There were a group of us — all friends together. John was one of them too.'

'So, you've known John since you were both very young too,' Isla said slowly. 'I hadn't realised that.'

'Yes, although John and I actually went to school together until we were eleven. We went our separate ways after college and met up at a reunion a couple of years after Tom and I divorced. Now, enough of this reminiscing. I fancy going into Tunbridge Wells to do some shopping if you want to come along.'

Isla decided to accept the offer. It

was time she bought some new clothes, although she couldn't afford to be too extravagant.

As she went upstairs to get ready, she reflected that her aunt had given her a lot to think about. She was beginning to realise she knew even less about her family history than she thought she did. There were many more questions she wanted to ask but decided that now wasn't the right time.

★　★　★

Saturday promised to be another glorious day. Isla and Amy were covering at Laburnum Cottage for the first couple of hours.

'It's good we've got this opportunity to talk. I was wondering if you'd like to come out for that pub meal on Wednesday.'

'Love to,' Isla told her. 'Providing you don't try to set me up on a blind date.'

Amy laughed. 'No, you've made that abundantly clear — there might just be a group of us, but there's safety in numbers!'

The time zipped past and there was no sign of Jed Rowley. At eleven thirty, Amy's mobile played a lively tune and she grabbed it from her pocket and spoke briefly.

'That was Mum, Isla, wanting to know if I can get over to Gardenia House; she's been covering for me but needs to be back at Ellen's place now.'

'It's a bit like musical chairs today, isn't it? Off you go, I'll be fine here for the time being, although goodness alone knows what's happened to Jed.'

'I'm right here' said a voice from the doorway. 'I'm so sorry, you two. Got held up at the barn. Have you had many visitors this morning?'

'A steady trickle. We've recorded any sales and taken someone's business card so that they can get in touch with you about a commission. Your mobile was switched off.'

Jed came into the room. 'Yes — there was a slight emergency in the kitchen.

One of the helpers burnt her hand so I needed to step in whilst a first aider sorted her out.'

'Is she OK?' Isla asked anxiously.

'Yes, thankfully, but it left us a helper short down there. Anyway, my father and Aunty June have volunteered their services.'

'Wow, that should be interesting,' Amy said, her eyes sparkling with amusement.

'What *do* you mean, Miss Bradshaw?' Jed asked with a straight face. 'They're both in their element. When I left, they were bossing everyone else about. My father has always fancied himself as a waiter and someone's found him a striped apron and draped a teacloth over his arm.'

Still grinning, Amy shot off to Gardenia House, leaving the pair of them to hold the fort.

'If you need to get back to John, I can manage here,' Jed told Isla.

'You can't cover all three rooms *and* be available to shoot off to sort out any hitches elsewhere,' she pointed out. 'I wouldn't mind grabbing a coffee though. Do you want one? The Franklins have left some refreshments for us in their kitchen and I'd just switched the kettle on.'

'Sounds like a good idea to me.'

Jed was pleased to see Isla looking more relaxed that morning. He realised she was very different from her aunt, both in looks and personality, and wondered how they got on. He had given Isla quite a hard time when they had first met and liked the way she had stood up to him, although he'd no intention of letting her know that.

A few minutes later, Isla returned, bearing a tray of coffee and chocolate biscuits.

There was a lull in visitors and Jed rummaged in his backpack and produced a bag. 'Sausage rolls, courtesy of the WI. They were meant to be for lunch but we might as well have them now before the next influx of visitors . . . '

He pulled up a chair and came to sit

beside her, stretching out his long, jean-clad legs. She was acutely aware of his presence. She could smell the musky scent of his cologne and see a shaft of sunshine streaking his fair hair with gold. She pulled herself together, determined not to fall for his charm.

★   ★   ★

Over lunch, Isla filled Jed in with the conversations she had had with visitors that morning.

'Sounds like you and Amy have been doing a brilliant job. The Franklins will be pleased. When they come back this evening, they'll need to replenish their stock for tomorrow . . . By the way, I popped in on John and his pottery demonstration was so popular that we've had an additional three people sign up for vacancies on his first course, should anyone drop out.'

'That's good, isn't it? He produces such lovely work.'

'And he's one of the most modest

chaps I know. He's sold a number of pieces this morning, and you've had another purchase too.' He shot a look at her and saw the slight tinge of pink on her cheeks and the little smile playing about her lips.

'Great! I needn't feel so guilty over the shopping I did the other day now.'

'Have you got any future plans, workwise? Apart from the summer school, I mean.'

'No. I'm giving myself a bit of a breather for a few weeks, but that doesn't mean to say I won't be on the look-out for anything that might come up. Unfortunately, I can't live on fresh air.'

One or two visitors had been wandering round and now came across to Jed. She registered that he had a very pleasant manner, taking time and trouble to answer their questions and as Amy had commented, he was very good-looking. She wondered where Nicole was that day; tied up with her own enterprises, she supposed.

'That couple were so interested — fired loads of questions at me,' Jed said, as he rejoined her. 'Although the Franklins won't get rich from their purchases — neither will I, for that matter.'

'Ah well, that isn't always the object of the exercise, is it? The ability to inspire people or give them a little pleasure from your artwork is also important.'

'Absolutely. That's why we promote the summer school during these events. There are usually a few spaces on several of the later courses, but most people signed up last year.'

'I like your work, but thought your prices were rather steep,' she told him honestly. 'Do you make many sales?'

He laughed, liking her straightforward manner. 'Is that a less-than-subtle way of indicating that, in your opinion, I should aim a bit lower?'

She coloured. 'I didn't mean — it's none of my business, but . . . '

'You're entitled to your opinion. As

I'm sure I don't need to tell you, tastes in art change. I might be able to command a good price for my creations at the moment, but probably, in a year or two, that won't be so. Actually, if you think about the time, effort and energy that go into an artist's work, then there's absolutely no need for any of us to feel guilty about any sales we make.'

Isla was tempted to reply that she would need to sell several paintings to get the sort of money he'd make from just one sale, but she bit her tongue.

The door flew open and Nicole came into the room. 'Oh, good, you are still here, Jed. Why on earth have you switched your phone off?' She completely ignored Isla.

'Hallo to you too . . . I've forgotten to switch it back on. It's been busy.'

'Looks like it,' Nicole said, eyeing the remains of their lunch. 'Fortunately, I ran into Amy Bradshaw just now at Gardenia House. She said you'd probably still be here.'

She crossed to Jed's side and put a

possessive hand on his shoulder. 'How are you doing? Have there been any sales?'

'Just an enquiry about a commission. I'm happy with that.'

'I should hope so. It sounds promising.'

Isla's mobile trilled. It was Ellen, asking if she would be able to return to Ivy Cottage, as she could do with an extra pair of hands at her place.

'Right, although I could still be needed here.'

She looked across at Jed and told him what Ellen had said, but before he could speak, Nicole told her, 'I'm here to help Jed now, so off you go,' and gave her a look that spoke volumes.

'Thanks so much for your help,' Jed said. Feeling slightly piqued, Isla collected up her bag and left. She couldn't explain to herself why she was put out by the sight of Nicole standing so close to Jed. Why on earth should it matter to her? She barely knew the man.

Ellen was looking pleased with herself when Isla arrived at Ivy Cottage. 'Nicole Trent called in looking for Jed,' Ellen told her. 'She's delighted with Christina's work and, of course, I was able to thank Nicole personally for the flowers. And guess what? She's bought three more cushions from me. As you know, I put two on display from the sofa in the spare room, and she asked me if I happened to have a third. I took the one from your room.'

Isla didn't know whether to be amused or annoyed. She had admired the cushion, and Ellen had told her she could keep it, so she'd taken it into her bedroom.

'I liked that cushion,' she told her aunt, and waited for her to accuse her of being petty.

'Oh, I'll make you another one, but it would have been silly to let an opportunity like that slip through my fingers. There's no sentiment in business, as I've told you before. Nicole offered me a good price. That's the difference between you and me, Isla; I'm afraid you don't have a very good head for business.'

Isla shrugged, not for the first time recognising that Ellen and herself viewed things differently. Personally, Isla had thought her aunt had been rather ruthless when selling so many of Gran's possessions on eBay. She had realised then that Ellen was not in the least sentimental, unlike herself, who treasured things that her aunt would consider to be rubbish.

'Nicole has style,' Ellen went on now. 'She certainly knows how to make the best of herself — beautiful hair and make-up — real panache.'

'I expect she has a job that requires her to dress like that, unlike us artists who have a uniform of jeans and t-shirts,' Isla pointed out, tongue in cheek.

'Mmm, but it doesn't hurt to make an effort now and then' Ellen told her pointedly, and not for the first time.

6

Isla spent the next hour or so at Ivy Cottage and then, at Ellen's suggestion, went along to the workshop to see how John was getting on.

When she arrived, she found him deep in conversation with a large stocky man with bright brown eyes, longish light brown hair and a beard.

'Hi, Isla. Come and meet Sam Westfield. You'll be working alongside him at Rowley Grange while I'm in New Zealand.'

They exchanged greetings and Sam engulfed her hand in his. She liked him on sight and was relieved to find he seemed as easy going as John.

'My wife, Mollie, would love your paintings. Unfortunately, she suffers from rheumatoid arthritis and is having a bad day so couldn't come, but she insisted I did because we missed out last time.'

'Oh, perhaps we can find a way round it on another occasion,' Isla told him sympathetically. 'My grandmother has arthritis so I realise how painful it can be.'

Sam nodded. 'Her sister-in-law is with her at the moment. I was hoping to catch up with Jed Rowley. I wanted to have a few words about the summer school, but when I saw him earlier, he was with his lady friend, Nicole, and it didn't seem the right moment to bend his ear.'

'I know he wants to speak with the three of us at some point,' John told him. 'I expect he'll be in touch to finalise a few details.'

'Ellen tells me Nicole Trent has panache,' Isla said naughtily, and waited for John's reaction. She wasn't disappointed.

'Good gracious, that sounds nasty — is it contagious?' he asked, keeping a straight face but with a twinkle in his eye.

'John's always had a wicked sense of humour,' Sam said, when they'd stopped laughing. He then added perceptively, 'She is an attractive woman, but it's surprising what expensive clothes can do.'

The last few visitors, who had been up the church tower and then had tea, appeared at that point. John went to talk to them, and Isla was about to excuse herself and join them when Sam said something which caught her attention.

'Of course, John and I go back a long way.'

'Yes, I gather you were at Art College together.'

Sam rubbed his chin. 'No, I've actually known him longer than that — from when we were eleven, as a matter of fact. We were at grammar school together. It was actually my cousin, Tom Westfield, who was at Art College with him . . . '

He trailed off as Isla cut across him. '*Tom Westfield*! But he was my Aunt Ellen's first husband. I thought your surname rang a bell, and now I know why. No-one told me you were his cousin.'

Sam looked embarrassed. 'No, well, perhaps I oughtn't to have mentioned it. Look, forget I said anything. I gather it's a bit of a taboo subject.'

'Mmm. As I've got older, I've realised that — although Ellen did mention Uncle Tom briefly the other day when we were discussing something. Anyway, I don't understand the problem. Lots of people have been married more than once.'

'Yes, but you see, John was Tom's best man,' Sam said.

'Really!' Isla's mind began to work overtime. 'I was only small when Aunt Ellen and Uncle Tom divorced. He was kind to me, and I missed seeing him around. I must have been about fourteen when I heard that he'd died.'

Sam hesitated before replying. 'Yes, it was a shock to all of us when he suffered that heart attack. Anyway, best not dwell on the past. Sorry if I've spoken out of turn.'

Isla shook her head emphatically. 'I can assure you, you haven't. It's fascinating to discover someone related to Uncle Tom.'

Just then, John beckoned to her, and, excusing herself to Sam, she went across to speak to an elderly couple about her paintings.

★   ★   ★

Isla found it difficult to sleep that night and found herself reflecting on what Sam had told her. She had learnt more about her family from him in those few minutes than she had in all her twenty-nine years.

She remembered the conversation she'd overheard between John and her grandmother when they'd visited her in Bexhill. Isla had no idea what had caused the break-up of her aunt's marriage, and it was hardly the kind of question she could ask Ellen or John. She wondered if Sam knew.

★   ★   ★

'Would it be an idea if I took my lunchbreak now?' Isla asked John, as it approached one o'clock on Sunday.

'What?' John was utterly engrossed in the bowl he was decorating.

Isla repeated her question, patiently adding, 'Only I've promised to be at Laburnum Cottage around two.'

John looked up briefly. 'Oh yes, you cut along, by all means.'

'Are you intending to close for lunch, or shall I fetch you something back?'

'Mmm? Oh, don't worry about me. I'll finish what I'm doing here and then close up for a short while. It's fairly quiet just now. Ellen wants me to look in at home. Says I ought to show an interest in what everyone else is doing.'

Isla thought that was rich, seeing how, as far as she was aware, her aunt hadn't been anywhere near John's workshop. She smiled, seeing that he'd become totally absorbed in creating his bowl once more. She stepped out into the sunshine.

Sunday was proving to be very much

a repeat of Saturday, except that she was able to spend more time with John at the workshop because Dale was helping out at Laburnum Cottage during the morning.

She suddenly remembered she'd told Penny she'd endeavour to find time to climb the church tower and decided it would make sense to do that before eating.

It was quite a steep climb up the winding staircase. When she reached the top, she was astonished to encounter Jed Rowley leaning on the edge of the tower and admiring the view. She watched him for a moment or two, waiting for him to notice her. She wondered if he was gaining inspiration for another piece of work.

'Hi,' she said softly, moving to his side.

He turned around at the sound of her voice, a faraway look in his eyes. Her heartbeat quickened. She had to admit that he had the sort of looks that could turn a girl's head — not that she had

116

any intention of letting that happen.

He pushed back a strand of hair that had fallen across his forehead and smiled.

'Hallo again. Wonderful spot this,' he said. 'It brings meaning to those words *I'm feeling on top of the world*.'

She nodded and smiled back, and they stood there for a few moments looking at the patchwork of fields; they looked like one of Ellen's quilts. She could see a herd of Friesian cattle grazing in the distance, what she supposed was the farmhouse and, beyond, some oast houses. It was a tranquil scene.

Presently, they moved round and looked from the opposite side. Jed noted the look of rapture on her face as she surveyed the scene below.

'Oh, are those the grounds of Rowley Grange?'

'Yes, and if you look over there you can just make out the Arts Centre where we'll be holding the summer school.'

'Where? The only building I can see apart from the vicarage is something that looks like a village hall — red brick and probably Victorian.

'That's because it's exactly what it used to be. A few years back when the barn was renovated, the village hall became a bit of a spare part. But then my father had the brilliant idea of using it as an Arts Centre, so he purchased it. Of course, it's used for other things too or it wouldn't be viable.'

'But it's not being used for exhibitions this weekend.'

'No, it needed a few repairs and some redecorating to get it ready for the summer school. And anyway, people enjoy visiting the artists in their own homes for these events. Now, if we move a bit further along here and you look over to your right . . . ' He rested a hand lightly on her shoulder to point her in the right direction, and she caught her breath at his touch; it seemed to send little shivers dancing along her spine.

118

'See, just behind that group of trees is the Manor.'

'Oh, yes, I can just make out the chimneys. The sort that artists itch to draw because they're all so individual. Do any of the residents from the home manage to get to the open weekends?'

'A few of the fittest. Sometimes it's easier to bring the world to them. I try to pop in now and again, and some of the other members of the Art Society do the same.'

'To talk with them, you mean?'

'Yes, but some of them enjoy a hands-on painting or craft session. Clay work can be a bit messy, but they love to decorate ready-made mugs and bowls. John, Sam and I took a workshop there not long ago. It was really rewarding. We thoroughly enjoyed it and hopefully, they did too.'

'That sounds interesting. I must ask John to tell me about it. He's never mentioned it, but that's typical of John.'

She was beginning to learn things about this man by her side, too. She had obviously misjudged him when they first met. It was good that he was prepared to give his time to visit the more senior and less mobile members of society and involve them in creative projects.

Some other visitors arrived at the top of the stairs and reluctantly she moved along to make more space. Suddenly, something else caught her attention. The sun glinted on water in the distance, striking it silver.

'Oh, is that a river I can see in the distance — beyond those trees?'

'It's a brook, actually. It's a picturesque place, but on private land.'

'So, who does it belong to?' she asked curiously.

'My father. It's part of the Rowley Grange estate now, but it used to belong to the Manor. When the previous owners sold it about a decade ago the people who bought the Manor didn't want all the land; some was purchased for a conservation area and picnic spot, but the brook and the little bridge over it were bought by my father. Actually, it's supposed to be the bridge that gave Woodbridge its name, although I would have thought it's highly unlikely to be the same one.'

'That's fascinating,' Isla murmured.

'I'll show you one day, if you're interested, although it's quite a walk. It's a wonderful spot.'

'You've whetted my appetite. Sounds a wonderful spot for a painter too.'

'Absolutely. I've heard it referred to as a painters' paradise. Are you ready to go back down now?'

She consulted her watch. 'Oh, my goodness. I'm supposed to be at Laburnum Cottage around two, and I haven't had any lunch yet. It's all so interesting up here.'

'Yes, I always make a point of coming up here when I get the opportunity.'

As they made their way carefully back down the winding staircase and into the church once more, Isla had to admit to herself that she had enjoyed the time she'd spent with Jed. He turned to help her down the final step, and again a little frisson trembled along her spine at the touch of his fingers on hers. Another group of people were waiting to ascend to the tower and Jed greeted them pleasantly.

Nicole was waiting impatiently on the bench as they emerged into the sunshine.

'I thought you'd gone for the duration, Jed,' she complained. 'Your father told me where he thought you'd be, and then I could see the pair of you up there on the roof.'

She made it sound as if they'd been up to no good, Isla thought.

'You could have come to find me,' Jed said mildly.

Nicole shuddered. 'You know how I hate heights.'

'What a pity, it's a wonderful view up there,' Isla told her. 'You can see for miles around.'

Nicole's grey eyes narrowed. 'Really. I prefer to stay on *terra firma*, thanks. The rural scene doesn't do a lot for me.' She brushed a ladybird from her skirt.

'Nicole is more comfortable in a town or city,' Jed informed Isla, and turned to the woman perched on the bench. 'You'd miss the buzz if you lived around here, wouldn't you?'

'I certainly would, but to be fair I'm very supportive of events like this. Ellen Ainsworth is quite a find, and through her I've been put in touch with Christina, who is going to prove invaluable . . . So are you coming back to the Grange for lunch, Jed? Your father says there's smoked salmon left over from yesterday evening's meal and salad to go with it.'

He shook his head. 'Sounds tempting, but sorry — no can do. I'm needed elsewhere shortly. Let's grab something at the barn. I'm sure the WI ladies have got some quiche or . . . '

'Sausage rolls,' Isla suggested, and saw the twinkle in Jed's eyes. 'That's where I'm off to right now.'

'Well, each to his own.' Getting to her

feet, Nicole tucked her arm through Jed's. 'Tell me where you'll be, and I'll rustle up some smoked salmon sandwiches; although I don't see why you can't take some time-out — after all, you've got enough minions to do all that running around for you.' She directed a little smile at Isla as she said this.

Inwardly fuming, Isla bit back a sharp retort. Catching Jed's gaze, she saw the glint in his eyes and was almost certain he hadn't liked the remark either.

'Well, this minion needs to get off now, before they run out of sausage rolls!' she said lightly, determined not to let Nicole see how her remark had affected her. She hurried off in the direction of the barn, wondering why she'd let the older woman get under her skin. She knew it was irrational.

It was obvious that Nicole had only come to the open weekends to suit her own ends. Isla supposed there was nothing wrong with that but couldn't imagine Nicole doing anything without a motive. It was obvious that Jed loved the rural life and a pity that she didn't share his enjoyment of the countryside and local affairs. Isla supposed that if their relationship became serious, Nicole would probably talk him into moving to the city. The thought disturbed Isla and she told herself sternly that that was irrational too.

When Isla arrived at Laburnum Cottage, it was to find Jane Bradshaw there with her other daughter Allyson, speaking with a young couple and their son, who Isla had encountered earlier at the workshop. Jane waved a hand in greeting and, grinning, pointed at her small granddaughter, Skye, who was proudly showing them her own picture.

After a minute or two, Jane intervened, suggesting that the children went into the garden whilst the grown-ups had a look at the exhibitions.

'Come on, Tyler, I'll show you the metal birds and other thingummies,' Skye told the little boy importantly.

'What sort of thingummies?' Tyler asked, screwing up his small, freckled face.

Skye put her hands on her hips. 'Well, I don't know what they are s'posed to be, do I? That's why I call them thingummies. You have to use your 'magination. Come on.'

And she charged off into the garden, the little boy following on behind.

'She's a caution, isn't she?' Tyler's father commented.

'Mmm. Seven going on twenty-seven, I think sometimes,' Allyson said with a grin.

Shortly afterwards, Jerome Rowley put in an appearance. 'I'm reporting for duty. I'm standing in for Jed whilst he and Nicole have some lunch. She was a bit insistent. Don't think she's used to this sort of set-up.'

Isla gave him a knowing look. 'Obviously not. Actually, we've had that conversation already. I understand she's not keen on rural life.'

He shrugged. 'It would seem she's not heavily into parochial affairs either, but does appear to be keen on my son. Now, tell me what I can do around here. I'm a dab hand at washing up and making tea.'

Jerome's words hit home. Up until that morning, she'd still hoped that Nicole Trent really was *just* a friend of Jed's, but Isla had reluctantly realised she'd been kidding herself. The older woman was obviously a great deal more than that.

☆　☆　☆

Isla spent the last part of the afternoon back at the workshop and just before it finally drew to a close, the door opened to admit Jerome Rowley.

'I'm absolutely delighted with the way these two open weekends have turned out. They've been a rip-roaring success. Now, did you two get the message about our get-together at the pub around seven? I've twisted the chef's arm and he's agreed to do a special carvery in our honour. Everyone's invited — my treat, and I don't intend to take no for an answer.'

'Well, in that case, we'll be happy to

accept,' John told him with a grin.

When he'd gone, Isla said, 'I'm not sure about this, John. After all, I am only an associate member and only that by default.'

'Nonsense, you're part of us now and don't you forget it! Like Jerome Rowley, I don't intend to take *no* for an answer.'

Isla realised that one of the reasons she didn't want to go to the meal that evening was that she wasn't at all keen to run into Nicole Trent again. That young woman rubbed her up the wrong way with her airs and graces.

When she and John got back to Ivy Cottage, Ellen surveyed the pair of them and said, 'I think we need to make ourselves look presentable for this do tonight.'

John shrugged. 'Painting and pottery aren't the cleanest occupations. I don't think the others will bother too much about dressing up.'

Ellen sniffed. 'Even so, sometimes it doesn't hurt to make an effort.'

John and Isla exchanged slightly amused glances as they made their way towards the stairs. Having showered, Isla changed into a denim skirt and one of the new tops she'd bought on the recent shopping trip in Tunbridge Wells. She brushed her hair, swept it into a neat ponytail and applied some light make-up. She wasn't sure why she was making an effort, but at least her aunt would be pleased.

To Isla's relief, there was no sign of Nicole Trent when they got to the pub, but Jed wasn't there either. She felt ridiculously disappointed. The members of the Woodbridge Art Society were a friendly crowd and she soon relaxed in their company. She knew quite a few of them already and John introduced her to the rest.

'Dominic tells me you'll be involved in the summer school this year,' said a red-haired lady, wearing a flowing dress in vivid shades of orange and red.

'Yes, a couple of painting courses, but I'll be helping out with John's pottery too.'

'That's great. During the few years

they've been running, they've proved a great success. They've really got off the ground. Of course, Dom's such a good organiser. I wonder where he and Jed have got to. I'm starving.'

As if on cue, the door swung open and Jed appeared, followed by Dominic Irwin.

'Good! Now everyone's here, we can go into the restaurant.' Jerome Rowley said. 'We were beginning to think you two had got lost.'

'Just ironing out a couple of details about the summer school whilst we had the opportunity,' Jed told his father.

Everyone collected their glasses and went to a side room where a large round table had been laid up in readiness for them.

'Shades of King Arthur,' Amy murmured, and Isla smiled.

She found herself sitting in between Dominic and Dale Irwin and opposite Jed.

'What's happened to Nicole?' someone asked, and Isla pricked up her ears.

'Oh, she had a prior engagement up in town she couldn't get out of,' Jed said, and the waiter appeared at that moment to see if they needed any wine.

At that point, Isla relaxed and began to enjoy the evening. Dominic, she discovered, was not really serious at all. Now that he and Dale were sitting near each other, she could see the resemblance. They shared some of the same mannerisms and features, although their build and colouring were different. Whilst they waited to go up to the carvery, the two of them kept up a constant banter, causing those within earshot to laugh.

By the end of the meal, Dominic and Isla had discovered quite a bit about each other. They had some interests in common, such as their taste in music and films.

Jed, who was sitting next to the lady in the colourful dress, looked in their direction from time to time, but Isla pretended not to notice. Over coffee, Jerome Rowley made a short speech, thanking everyone for all their input during the open weekends.

'As ever, they have proved a resounding success,' Jerome told them. 'I had wondered how this year would work out, because I was unable to have my finger on the pulse as much as previously but, thanks to my son and Dominic, things couldn't have been better.'

Dominic looked serious again and a slight colour tinged his cheeks. Glancing at Jed, Isla saw he appeared to be studying his hands, but then his head shot up and he looked directly at her with a smile on his lips that sent her pulse racing.

'There's someone else I'd like to thank,' Jerome said. 'Someone who was thrown in at the deep end and took the challenge, and that's our new associate member — Isla Milne.'

There was a spontaneous round of applause and, after a moment or two, Jerome Rowley raised his hand for silence, a broad smile on his face.

'Isla has already proved to be an asset

to the group during these open week-ends, and I propose that she should be accepted as a full member of the Wood-bridge Arts Society.'

The decision was unanimous, and it was Isla's turn to feel embarrassed. She had been in Woodbridge such a short time, but already felt a part of the community.

'Thank you,' she mumbled, 'for making me feel so welcome.'

There was yet another round of applause and Jerome passed a badge across the table, which Dale obligingly pinned on to her top — his fingers lingering a little too long for her liking. As Isla smilingly thanked Jerome Rowley, she saw Jed watching, and this time it was his turn to look serious. She wondered what he was thinking; perhaps he wasn't as supportive of her being a full member as she'd supposed.

The evening drew to a close shortly afterwards, as several members had work on the following morning. Dominic got to his feet.

'It's been great getting to know you, Isla. I've thoroughly enjoyed this evening.'

'So have I,' she told him and shook the hand he extended warmly. If she had looked in Jed's direction, she would have seen the expression on his face as he watched the two of them. He reflected that Dominic Irwin wasn't wasting time making friends with their latest recruit and it irked him.

'I'll be in touch about Wednesday evening,' Amy told her.

'Wednesday evening?' Isla repeated, mystified.

'Yes, our get-together. You are still up for it?'

'Oh, yes, of course.'

'Great. I'll see you there then.'

Isla saw the impish smile on Amy's face and hoped she wasn't going to regret it.

'Well done,' John said, patting her on the shoulder. 'I'm proud of you. Told you she'd be an asset, didn't I Ellen?'

Ellen gave her a half-smile and

continued her conversation with Jane Bradshaw. Isla thought it wouldn't have hurt her aunt to have congratulated her.

Jed was standing by the bar as his father settled the bill. 'We'll need to arrange that meeting with Sam and John soon — by the end of this week, in fact,' he told Isla. 'I'll sort something out and let you know.'

'That's my son,' Jerome said. 'Finishes one project and straight onto the next.'

'You'd have something to say if I left it all in the air,' Jed told him. 'Come on, some of us have got homes to go to.'

'It was a lovely meal,' she told Jerome. 'Thank you for including me.'

'You're more than welcome, my dear. You're one of us now and I shall expect great things from you, young lady. You've got a lot of potential.'

She felt a warm glow inside her at this and hoped that she could live up to Jerome Rowley's expectations. She couldn't wait to tell her grandmother about the weekend, although some things she would choose to keep to herself.

7

Isla went to see her grandmother again on Tuesday. This time she went alone, but with a message from Ellen to say that she and John would be there at the weekend. Isla filled her gran in with what had been going on since she'd last visited.

'It's a bit confusing, isn't it?' Martha said. 'All those names. However do you sort out who's who? I have enough of a problem remembering what the folk who sit on my table at mealtimes are called. The fellow who sat next to you at that dinner sounds nice — Don, is it?'

'Dom, actually — short for Dominic. Don't go getting any ideas, Gran. He's Jerome Rowley's right-hand man, and so obviously he's taking an interest in me because I've been employed to help out at the summer school.'

Gran screwed up her face in concentration. 'Rowley — that name rings a bell.'

'Probably because I've been talking about the Rowleys on and off for a while now.'

Gran snapped her fingers. 'Got it! The niece of a friend of mine married a Rowley. I wonder if it was the same one.'

She'd captured Isla's imagination. 'Can you remember the niece's name? Perhaps John might know, or even Dom, if she was Jerome Rowley's wife.'

Gran thought for a moment, then shook her head. 'Regretfully not, and my friend, Hilda, isn't around anymore so I can't ask her. Might not even be the same family . . . By the way, have you — er — met Sam Westfield yet?'

Isla was definitely interested now. 'Yes, he seems very nice. He can only work part-time because his wife is disabled. I don't know if Jerome Rowley is a widower, but I expect Sam does. Anyway, how come you know Sam?' she asked casually, deciding not to mention her recent conversation with him. It would be interesting to know what Gran had to say.

For a moment, Martha Milne didn't reply. Then, she said airily, 'Oh, he's a friend of Ellen and John's. I've heard them talk about him . . . Now, did you bring me those toiletries I wanted? I'm practically out of talcum powder.'

Her grandmother had always been adept at changing the subject when she was getting herself into a tight corner, Isla reflected. Obviously, the elderly lady wasn't prepared to say any more, which was a pity because she had whet Isla's appetite.

Isla stayed for a little longer and when she got up to go, Gran kissed her cheek and said, 'You're a good girl, Isla. I just wish you could find yourself a nice young man. I feel it's my fault that you split up with Ewan.'

Isla took Gran's gnarled hand in hers, 'Of course it isn't. If you ask me, it was a blessing in disguise. Anyway, I like being single. My painting's taking off again; I've got some work lined up for the summer, and I'm enjoying life in Woodbridge.'

Gran's features relaxed. 'That is good news, love. As long as you're happy then that's all that matters.'

Just then, the carers appeared to get the residents ready for lunch. As Isla drove off to visit her previous neighbours, and collect some more of her belongings from their garage, she reflected that it was true what she had just told her grandmother. Ewan was becoming a distant memory. She was beginning to enjoy her new life in Woodbridge and the people she had met there. Dominic Irwin was a nice character and she'd enjoyed his company on Sunday. And then, of course, there was Jed Rowley.

She thought back to Sunday lunchtime and how they'd met at the top of the church tower. Fleetingly, she remembered the touch of his hand on her shoulder; the way his fingers had entwined with hers as he'd helped her down the last steep step. She pulled herself together sharply. Jed Rowley was off limits. He was already involved with Nicole Trent who, as Ellen had said, had *panache*. She was far more suited to Jed's way of life. Isla smiled ruefully as she accepted that, even if he had been free, he was unlikely to be interested in her except on a professional level.

⋆   ⋆   ⋆

When she arrived back at Ivy Cottage, John informed her that the meeting with Jed Rowley had been fixed for the following evening at five thirty. Apparently, it was the only time that suited everyone.

'I said I'd check with you but thought you'd be OK.'

It wasn't until she'd agreed that it was that she remembered she was going out with Amy and Dale that evening. She hoped the meeting wouldn't take too long.

Presently, Amy rang as promised to confirm arrangements. Isla explained about the meeting.

'Yes, I know. Dom mentioned it. He's going to give you a lift afterwards.'

'Dominic? But I can easily drive to yours if you give me directions.'

'That would be daft when you'll both be at the Grange beforehand.'

'Oh, yes, we will. It's going to be a bit of a rush. The meeting was arranged when I was out visiting Gran and, as I'm still very much the newcomer, I can't very well object. But won't I be taking Dominic out of his way?'

'No, Dale's asked him along too. Anyway, Dom will make sure the meeting doesn't overrun. So, no worries.'

Isla swallowed back a comment. It was obvious that Amy was determined to make up a foursome but after all, Isla reasoned, it was feasible that Dale would ask his brother to join them. They were a likeable pair and she'd enjoyed their company at the pub on Sunday.

'Right. Well, is it still a pub meal or what? Just so as I know what to wear.'

'Actually, we wondered about an Italian place we know. Nothing out of the ordinary, but good food. Just wear something summery.'

'Great. I love Italian. I'll look forward to it,' Isla told her new friend, and realised that she meant it. She was beginning to enjoy life again after the traumas of the past few months.

★   ★   ★

Isla was the first to arrive at Rowley Grange. She'd left John in the car dealing with a phone call. She was dressed for her evening out, in a cotton print dress in shades of pink and green. Her newly washed hair swung loose about her shoulders. Jed opened the door.

'Hallo, Isla. Come along in. Are you the advance party?'

'Yes, I didn't want to be late again. John will be along in a minute. He's just on the phone to a work colleague.'

She followed Jed into what she assumed was the dining-room and sat at the large mahogany table. Jed sat opposite and shuffled some papers. Suddenly, he looked up with a smile, and her heart missed a beat.

'I like your dress. Your hair's different, too. It suits you like that.'

She felt colour tinge her cheeks. 'Oh, thanks. I'm going out directly after this meeting. Amy Bradshaw and Dale Irwin have invited me.'

'Good. I'm glad you're making friends.' He turned his attention back to the papers in front of him.

Just then, the doorbell pealed. There was the sound of voices in the hall, and a moment or two later John and Sam came into the room, followed by Dominic Irwin carrying a coffee tray.

'Your father said to start, and he'll be along shortly,' he told Jed. 'He's just attending to something that can't wait.' He looked in Isla's direction and smiled.

As soon as they had received their coffee, the meeting began. It was business-like and Jed didn't waste any time in raising one or two issues.

'Isla doesn't know the ropes and so, as we've already discussed, it makes sense for her to sit in on a couple of sessions with the pair of you next week, just to get the feel of the way we work. I'm sure I can rely on you to fill her in — show her where the stock is kept, go through health and safety procedures, explain about breaks and catering arrangements, et cetera. She was, after all, initially only expecting to take the painting courses,' he said, pointedly.

John looked up. 'Yes, well, as I've told you, Isla has assured me she doesn't mind assisting Sam with the last pottery course, and we don't foresee any problems, Jed.'

Jed's eyes glinted. 'Except that you've got one or two returnees from last year who are expecting you to be their tutor,' he said meaningfully.

Isla thought they had got over that

hurdle, but obviously not. She hadn't counted on there being any of the students from the previous year.

John clicked his pen on an off and then said, 'Well, if they don't like it, they can always drop out, but they won't get a refund this late in the day, will they?'

'It depends on whether there's anyone on the waiting list. Anyway, leaving that aside, let's move on. Do you have any questions, Isla?'

'Are there just two courses running at a time?' she wanted to know.

'At present, yes. We don't have sufficient space to accommodate more than twenty or so students at any one time. Alice Mercer, who you've met during the Artists' open weekends, will be running a couple of courses on paper sculpture. I've already managed to speak with her. When you do your painting course, Isla, there will be someone else in the building in place of John and Sam, but I'll fill you in with that at a later date.'

Jerome Rowley came into the room just then, and there was a pause whilst he took his seat at the head of the table and Dominic poured him some coffee.

'Sorry folk — just received an email that needed answering there and then. What have I missed?' he wanted to know.

'Nothing important,' Jed assured him. 'I just want Isla to understand the way the courses here are run. I've explained that we're part of a team and all pull together, regardless of our individual expertise.'

'Yes, and we try to remember that, for some of the students, this is their holiday, so we endeavour to make their time here as enjoyable as possible,' Jerome added.

The first part of the meeting was on general matters, such as the need for equality and inclusion. A lot of what was said was routine and common sense, but Isla could understand why it was necessary to reinforce it.

Having dealt with that, Jed said,

'We've got around a dozen to fifteen residents for each course, as well as a few coming in daily. For Isla's benefit I'll explain that those who stay over are fixed up with B and B accommodation in and around Woodbridge.'

'What about their other meals?' Isla wanted to know.

'We order packed lunches from the bakery. On Sunday, when they arrive, those who wish to do so go to the pub for a meal. For the rest of the time, they either make their own arrangements or, if they prefer it, some very nice ladies from the village cook them a basic meal which they eat together in the dining-room at the centre. They need to book for that in the evening before.'

Jed then moved on to the next part of the meeting, which was concerned with the courses themselves and the exhibitions at the end of each week. Jed didn't waste any time and was obviously used to sorting things out. Isla admired the smooth and efficient manner in which he dealt with matters.

When the meeting finally wound up, it was still almost a quarter to seven. There were a number of questions Isla was burning to ask, but they would have to wait. Dominic had got to his feet and was looking across the table at her.

'Ready when you are, Isla.'

Isla nodded and reached for her jacket. Jed shot her a look and for some reason she felt uncomfortable. She told herself not to be ridiculous. Why would it matter to him if she went out with Dominic Irwin?

'Enjoy your evening, Isla. See you when I see you,' John said cheerfully as he picked up his file.

'Oh, are you off somewhere nice?' Jerome enquired.

'We're meeting up with my brother and Amy,' Dominic said airily, making it sound as if it was a cosy foursome. Well, Jed could think what he liked, she decided, shrugging on her jacket. Just for a moment she realised that she wished that he had been her partner for

149

the evening. In your dreams, she told herself sharply.

*　*　*

'That went well,' Jerome Rowley said, as he and Jed went to prepare their own supper. 'Isla Milne is a nice lass.'

Jed added pasta to a pan of boiling water and did not reply. He wasn't sure that he approved of Isla going out with Dominic Irwin, who had just recently broken up with his girlfriend.

Jerome saw the expression on his son's face. 'What's wrong, Jed?'

'Nothing — nothing at all.' After all, it wasn't his business, but Dominic Irwin seemed an unlikely match for Isla. Jed was only too aware that, whilst Dom was good at his job, his lifestyle left a lot to be desired. He had even had a dalliance with one of the students last year. He was a bit of a playboy and his relationships didn't seem to last too long. Jed got the impression that Isla wasn't the sort of girl to just be content with a casual affair and hoped Dominic would treat her well.

When Nicole rang later that evening to ask if he was free that weekend, he told her *no* rather sharply. As soon as he'd put the phone down, he felt guilty and rang back to say that he could take her out for a meal on Saturday evening, if she'd like that.

★　★　★

It was a fun-filled evening at Giovanni's. Isla felt her spirits lift. The Italian food was good and so was the wine. Dale and Dom were as good as any comedians, and Isla enjoyed herself so much that she was surprised to see how late it was getting.

'You can always stay over at mine,' Amy offered, when Isla mentioned it.

'I thought we might go on to a club,' Dominic said, exchanging looks with his brother.

'Some of us have work to go to in the morning,' Amy pointed out. Shortly

151

afterwards, she went off to freshen up and Isla joined her.

As soon as they were out of earshot, Amy said, 'I don't know what gets into those two when they get together. They seem to revert to being teenagers all over again.'

'They're good company, but they do seem to have been knocking back the wine.'

'They certainly have. It hasn't escaped my notice. Don't worry, Isla, if you want to get back to Woodbridge, I'll run you home. It's OK, we're using my car because Dale's has failed its MOT. Dom can leave his car here and I'll drop the pair of them back at mine en route.'

'But you've got work in the morning.'

'Yes, but actually I was being a bit economical with the truth. I've got a couple of free periods first thing and don't need to put in an appearance until after break, so no worries on that score.'

It had been a pleasant evening and, even though Dominic had seemed a bit crestfallen at the way it had ended, he had taken Isla's hand and planted a kiss on her cheek before they parted company. She decided she couldn't be cross with him for long but was grateful to Amy for rescuing her from a difficult situation. She hadn't fancied being alone with him.

'I've really enjoyed myself tonight, so thanks for inviting me,' she told Amy as she dropped her back at Ivy Cottage. 'I like Dom. He's good for a laugh, but I honestly don't think he's my type.'

Amy sighed. 'I don't think match-making is my forte; I think I'd better stick to my day job in the future!'

* * *

John still hadn't managed to find time to show Isla around the Arts Centre and the summer school was looming ever closer. On Friday, she went off to the village shop to make a few purchases for Ellen, who was at the hairdresser's. It was an amazingly well-stocked shop and, having located the kind of rice Ellen wanted, she was trying to reach it when an arm stretched up and dropped the packet in her basket.

Jed Rowley stood grinning down at her. 'Long arms come in useful sometimes.'

'Thanks. I didn't want to dislodge all those packets. I can't believe how much stuff is crammed into such a small amount of space. It's like Aladdin's cave in here.'

He grinned. 'Yes, it's surprising what you can find. Actually, I'm glad I've run into you . . . Has John shown you round the Arts Centre yet?'

'No, he keeps making excuses. He's very busy winding up his college courses but he'll break up soon.'

'Are you free right now?'

She glanced at her shopping basket. 'Well, there are a few things that ought to go straight in the fridge,' she said doubtfully, 'and Ellen might wonder where I've got to when she gets home from the hairdresser's.'

'Then how about I run you back to

Ivy Cottage — you deal with the shopping and leave a note for Ellen while I phone my father and tell him I'm giving you the guided tour.'

She smiled up at him, her heart beating absurdly fast. 'Sounds like a good plan to me. I really do want to see inside the building. Get the feel of the place before I start working there.'

A short while later, they pulled up in the car park at the rear of the Arts Centre.

Jed unlocked the door and Isla looked about her with interest. The old Victorian building had certainly been put to good use.

'These old buildings are usually quite spacious,' Jed commented as he led her inside. The hall itself had been divided into two rooms with a sliding screen.

'This is amazing,' she said, as she looked at the workbenches and the storage space along the back walls.

He showed her several other rooms which led off the main area; one of which was now used as a very pleasant dining-room, with a small but comfortable area at one end where the students could relax over a coffee. Leading off that room was a well-equipped office. Then there was a kitchen, sparkling with fresh paint and stainless-steel appliances. There was a cloakroom with lockers and beyond that, modern facilities specially designed to accommodate a wheelchair if necessary.

'I'm impressed,' Isla told him. 'So, what about the kiln for the pottery?'

'One of the workshops houses a couple of kilns, but remember that many of the students, in the first course, are complete beginners. These courses aren't long enough to do more than give them a taster. As we've already discussed, they can't do anything too ambitious in the given time'

'Well no, but they can certainly get to learn the basics — coil pots, pinch pots. They can make pendants and other small items and perhaps even have a go on the wheel, just for the sheer experience.'

He nodded. 'We give them demonstrations and one or two lectures in the evenings. We hope that they will be sufficiently encouraged and confident to continue at evening classes. We plan to run some here in the autumn.'

'John says that those who are local can come back when their stuffs been fired and try their hand at glazing and decorating on one of his Saturday courses.'

'Yes, but we also let them practise on items that have already been fired. We buy some in. They can decorate ready-made egg cups and mugs if they so wish.'

'Goodness, you've got it all worked out,' she said in admiration. 'Do you take some of the evening classes?'

'Usually, but the centre's been out of commission for a few weeks.'

Back in the hall, Isla studied some photographs on a wall board from the previous year. The work shown there was obviously from more advanced students.

'Oh, those are returnees,' Jed told her. 'Of course, some of the more advanced students are from John's college. They come along to finish and decorate their work, and to practise and add to their skills.'

As they left the building, he asked, 'Did it meet up to your expectations, then?'

'Absolutely.' She swallowed, suddenly feeling apprehensive. She just hoped she'd meet up to everyone else's, especially Jed's.

8

'I've been meaning to ask you about Wednesday evening,' Jed said, as he locked the door to the Arts Centre.

'I thought the meeting went well,' she told him.

His green eyes swept her face. 'Come on, I wasn't asking about the meeting, Isla, as you know full well.'

She coloured slightly. 'Oh, you mean my evening out with Amy, Dom and his brother. Yes, it was very enjoyable. They're good company.'

'I thought Dominic seemed a little worse for wear on Thursday,'

'Really? I expect he was just tired,' she said lightly, determined not to let Jed know what had happened.

Jed had stopped in his tracks, hands in pockets. 'Dominic can be a bit of a livewire,' he said slowly.

She stared at him. 'I'm aware of that,

Jed. He's fun-loving and enjoys life, which in my opinion is better than taking it too seriously.'

Jed wasn't to know that even if she hadn't enjoyed the evening, she would have had no intention of telling him. He was looking at her in a disapproving manner, which made her feel uncomfortable and as if she was in the wrong for going out with Dominic Irwin.

'Thanks so much for showing me round the Arts Centre. I can visualise where I'll be working now. I'm sure you must have a lot to do so don't trouble to drive me back — I'll enjoy the walk,' she told him awkwardly.

'Oh, it's no problem. I've got a few things to drop off at home, and my father was hoping you'd come in for a cup of tea. He'd enjoy another chat with you if you've got the time; he'd obviously like to know what you make of the Arts Centre.'

Put like that, she could hardly refuse. It almost sounded like a royal command.

She smiled at him and accepted

graciously, adding, 'Although I'm afraid I'm hardly dressed for afternoon tea.'

He laughed and surveyed her. 'I'm not taking you to the Ritz, Isla.' You look fine as you are. I like the casual look. After all, as I've said before, you are an artist.'

She coloured under his gaze and he couldn't help comparing her with Nicole who would dress up to the nines even if she was only working from home. He didn't think she possessed anything without a designer label. He preferred Isla's natural look. She wore virtually no make-up that day and her hair was escaping from the scrunchie so that silky tendrils swept her cheeks. He wanted to stretch out and touch them.

As he ushered Isla into the hall at the Grange a few minutes later, he said, 'You won't be seeing Dom today because he's off on a course.'

'I wasn't expecting to,' she told him sharply, and was gratified to note that he was the one to look uncomfortable now.

She wasn't expecting Jed to stay for tea either. This time he took her into the sitting-room, where his father was immersed in the crossword from his daily newspaper.

'Hi, Dad! Look who I've brought home for tea.'

Jerome looked up with a smile, 'Hallo Isla. I hoped you'd drop by to brighten up my otherwise uneventful day.'

There was a tabby cat curled up on a cushion on the sofa. It gave a homely touch.

'Hope you don't mind cats, Isla,' Jed said. 'This is Tabitha. Behave yourself, Tabs.'

Much to Isla's amusement, the cat opened one eye and meowed. Isla crossed the room and tickled her under her chin.

'Oh, I like cats. My grandmother had one for years. Unfortunately, it died about a year back.'

'Can you make the tea, Jed? I'm dying of thirst,' Jerome ordered.

Jed saluted. 'At the double, Sir,' he quipped.

The moment he'd gone, Jerome patted the chair nearest to him. 'Come and sit down and tell me what you think of the Arts Centre.'

She sat beside him and said candidly, 'I think it's amazing, but until I'm actually working there, I can't give you a proper answer. You see, I need to get the feel of the place first, as a working environment.

He nodded his approval. 'That's a very honest answer. In other words, the proof of the pudding is in the eating.'

He was an interesting person to talk to, Isla decided, as he enthused about the Arts Centre and how it had come into being. He reminded her of her grandfather, although Jerome was probably still only in his sixties.

'I've hung your painting in my bedroom — at least Jed has. I like your style, Isla. I love your use of colour. Actually, I've got a proposition to put to you.'

She stared at him questioningly, wondering what on earth he was going to ask her.

'How would you feel about taking on a commission? I'd like you to do a painting of Rowley Grange.'

'Really? But surely someone's already done that.'

He grimaced. 'Indeed, they have. There are a couple of dark, gloomy oil paintings in the entrance hall that don't do it justice, but I want something that makes it come alive and it's my belief you're just the person to do that.'

She coloured. 'I'd love to, if you think I could produce what you want,' she breathed excitedly.

'I wouldn't ask you if I didn't. I like what I've seen of your work and we can have a talk about this when you're not so busy. I realise you've got the summer school coming up.'

'I could do some preliminary sketches and take some photographs,' she told him, enthusiastically, eyes shining. 'It would be a pity to miss those wonderful yellow roses tumbling over the porch.'

'That's settled then. Feel free to come up whenever you like. Jed knows I wanted to approach you; we've already discussed it and he thinks it's a good idea.'

They were putting the world to rights when Jed appeared with a laden tray.

'Our cleaning lady, Gemma, keeps us supplied with scones and cake.' Jed explained.

'She makes a mean apple pie, too,' Jerome put in.

To Isla's secret delight, Jed poured the tea, handed round the scones and then sat down. She had wondered if he would stay. She helped herself to strawberry jam and bit into the scone appreciatively. Isla had never heard Jed call his father *Dad* before, and she realised that in the inner sanctum of their sitting-room, Jed and Jerome Rowley behaved far more informally, and it was good to see.

It was a beautiful, gracious room in tones of green and old gold, with comfortable sofas and side tables, and several pieces of antique walnut furniture gleaming from frequent polishing.

'I've asked Isla about the painting and she's agreed to do it,' Jerome told his son.

'That's good. There's no timescale, so take your time,' Jed said. He noted how Isla's eyes lit up as she enthused for a few minutes about the painting. He could tell that she was passionate about her work. She really was an attractive young woman. It was a pity she was becoming involved with Dominic Irwin. He was a playboy if ever Jed had met one and he hoped Isla wouldn't be hurt.

The conversation inevitably turned to the summer school but, after a while and almost without Isla realising it, Jerome gently swung it back to Isla.

'So, your grandmother still lives in Bexhill?' asked Jerome.

'Yes, in a residential home. She's not been there long.'

Jerome set down his cup and saucer and looked at her. 'I've got a feeling someone mentioned that she used to live not far from here a number of years ago.'

'Yes, we moved to Bexhill when I was very small.'

She wondered why he was so interested. Perhaps he was aware that her grandmother might know a family member of his, or had Sam mentioned that his cousin, Tom Westfield, had been Ellen's first husband?

'Do you happen to remember the name of the place where you used to live?' he asked now, studying her intently.

Isla thought for a moment wrinkling her brow in concentration. 'Barns something, I believe.'

'Barns Cross?' Jed prompted

'Yes, I think that was it. Is it very near here?'

'Oh, around five miles or so away. Were you actually born there?'

'Well, I was born in hospital, but we lived with my grandparents and, as far as I understand, that was in a small village called Barns Cross. Why, do you have any family there?'

'I used to at one time, but we're no

longer in touch. I suppose your grandmother might have known them.'

Jed was watching her closely now and a prickle ran along her spine. She took a deep breath. 'When I visited my grandmother earlier this week, she did happen to mention that when she'd lived there a friend of hers, who has since died, had a daughter who married a Rowley. Unfortunately, she couldn't remember the daughter's name.'

She thought Jerome looked relieved and wondered why.

'It's a small world,' Jed remarked. He cut some generous slices of coffee and walnut cake and passed the plate to her. When she had helped herself, he asked casually, 'Did your Aunt Ellen live at Barns Cross too?'

So, this was what all these questions were about. They were interested in Aunt Ellen. Sam must have mentioned his cousin, Tom, to them. Well, there wasn't a great deal to be said so Ellen couldn't accuse her of being indiscreet.

She swallowed a mouthful of cake.

'She did until she went to Art College. She attended a school in the area, but she got married before I was born — straight after she got her qualifications. Then she and her husband moved away to Surrey.'

This time, she decided to ask one or two questions of her own. 'Did much of your family live at Barns Cross?'

She was convinced she saw Jerome exchange a look with his son.

'Oh, at one time, yes, but there aren't many Rowleys around now, are there, Jed?'

'Not so far as I'm aware, although we haven't delved too deeply into our family tree.'

They lapsed into silence for a minute or two. Suddenly Jed's mobile rang and with a muttered apology he went from the room.

'More tea?' Jerome enquired.

'No, thanks. That was delicious.' She set her tea things on the tray.

Tabitha jumped down from the sofa and entwined herself round Isla's legs, purring loudly. Isla stooped to stroke her.

'She's taken to you,' Jerome remarked. 'Jed has captured her beautifully in bronze — over there, look, on the lamp table.'

Isla got up and went to look at the delightful little sculpture. She was still admiring it when Jed came back into the room.

'That was Nicole reminding me that we're going to the opera on Friday. I'd clean forgotten.'

Jerome pulled a face. 'You're welcome. I prefer a good old-fashioned musical myself. How about you, Isla?'

'Oh, I um — I'm not a very good judge because I can only actually remember going to one opera and that was years ago. Actually, I do enjoy some musicals. Thank you so much for the tea; it was delicious. I'd best be getting back to Ivy Cottage. I'll enjoy the walk, now that you've shown me the short cut, Jed.'

'Mind if I join you?' he asked casually. 'I've just remembered I need to collect my latest project from my workshop.

She could hardly refuse, and she knew that she didn't want to. She said her goodbyes to Jerome Rowley, and they set off through the little copse again, but this time they took a slightly different route. A couple of times he touched her arm: once to point out a couple of squirrels scampering up an oak tree, and again to show her a patch of foxgloves. Each time the contact sent her heart racing.

'This is such a lovely spot,' she told him, and meeting his eyes, she saw that she had pleased him. All too soon they had come to the gate leading into the churchyard, and a few minutes later, went through the lychgate and in the direction of the workshops.

'I've been wondering what the other workshops were used for.'

'Well, as I explained earlier — and I expect John has pointed out already — one of them houses the kiln. Another is shared by a couple of the other local artists and then there's mine, which is in a separate building, and was actually the old coach-house. You can take a peek, if you like.'

She did like. Deciding that another ten minutes wouldn't matter, she followed him along the narrow track, admiring his rear view in the snugly fitting jeans.

'So are the commissions you get mainly for pets?' she asked presently.

He nodded, 'Usually, although sometimes for children and adults too.'

The coach-house was slightly larger than John's converted stable and beautifully equipped. Unlike John's workshop, it was also extremely tidy. Jed disappeared through an archway and emerged presently, holding the sculpture he had just finished. He set it down carefully on the table and she gazed at it, enraptured. It was obviously a red setter and he had captured it perfectly. She reached out a finger and gently stroked it along the spine. The tail looked feathery, just as it would be in real life.

They were standing so close that she

was very aware of him. She could smell the woody scent of his cologne, and again recognised that this man attracted her.

There was a gleam in his green eyes as he said 'So, what do you think?'

'It's amazing, but aren't you afraid of someone getting in here and stealing it?'

'Well, it's a chance we have to take, but the building's alarmed and there's a safe.'

All too soon, it was time for her to return to Ivy Cottage. She had enjoyed the afternoon and she knew that she had enjoyed being in Jed Rowley's company most of all. For a moment, she wondered what it would be like if she were going to the opera with him on Friday instead of Nicole. She visualised herself in the elegant sea-green dress that she had seen in a boutique window recently. It had a low-cut bodice and shoe-string straps. On her feet she would have silver sandals made of fine leather. She would sweep her hair up high and wear more make-up than usual.

Isla came down to earth with a bang when she arrived back at Ivy Cottage and Ellen demanded crossly, 'Wherever have you been? And what's happened to the mushrooms I asked you to get?'

'I did text you to say I was going to tea with Jerome Rowley, and then Jed invited me to look round his workshop. As for the mushrooms, I'm afraid Roy's run out and there won't be any more until tomorrow.'

Ellen gave a little shrug of impatience. 'Typical! Oh, well, it can't be helped, I suppose. Can you wash some salad potatoes and prepare some celery?'

'Did you know Jed's workshop used to be the old coach house?' Isla asked, as she filled a bowl with water.

'Well, of course. It belonged to Rowley Manor once. Jed chose the biggest building for himself. But then if you're as loaded as the Rowleys, I suppose you can have exactly what you choose.'

Isla stared at her. 'But I understood

the Art Society purchased the stable block from the previous owners of Rowley Manor.'

'They did, but Jerome Rowley bought the Coach House from them outright for Jed.'

'So, are they very well off?' Isla asked.

'Oh, come on, you've only got to take a look at that house they live in to figure that one out. Anyway, it's no good standing here gossiping, or we won't get any supper tonight.'

Ellen had given Isla a lot to think about. Sadly, she realised that she and Jed Rowley lived in totally different worlds. She couldn't even begin to imagine what it would be like to be so wealthy.

*   *   *

A few days later, Isla found herself at a loose end and took herself to Tunbridge Wells again. She needed some art materials so that she could make a start on her painting of Rowley Grange. She had already made one or two preliminary sketches and taken a series of photographs but hadn't run into either Jed or Jerome on her visits to the Grange. It was good to have a project, she decided.

She was wandering down in the direction of The Pantiles when Dominic Irwin came out of an antique shop opposite. She hadn't seen much of him since the evening at the pub. He stared at her in astonishment.

'Isla! What are you doing here?'

'I was just about to ask you the self-same question. I'm shopping; are you selling the family silver?'

To her surprise, he coloured. 'Something like that. My brother desperately wanted to raise some cash to take Amy away for a couple of days for her birthday. I've managed to get him a few bob by getting rid of some stuff he was left by our grandfather.'

'That's a pity, if it was a family heirloom,' she remarked.

Dominic spread his hands. 'Hmm,

well Dale's not sentimental. I wish he'd do his own dirty business, but he's had to go on some training day, and he needs to pay for this mini break by tomorrow. Anyway, I'm actually meeting up with Jed presently for a business seminar. I've got time for coffee before then, if you have.'

They were sitting over coffee and cake in an old-world tea shop with low oak beams and prints of Tunbridge Wells in bygone eras on its walls, when he leant across the table.

'Isla, about the other evening . . . '

She raised her eyebrows. 'What about it? I enjoyed myself,' she told him with a grin.

He heaved a sigh. 'Phew that's all right then. Amy gave us a right ear-bashing about our behaviour when she returned from driving you home.'

'Well, you were a little exuberant and inebriated,' she said, surveying him sternly, her head on one side. 'Neither of you were in a fit state to drive, and that was a little unfair on Amy because she had to go to work the following morning.'

Dominic looked chastened. 'Yes, point taken. So, I suppose you won't consider coming out with me again?'

'It wasn't a date, Dom,' she told him gently.

'No, but if I promised to be on my best behaviour, would you give me a second chance?'

'Possibly — if it was the right occasion.'

'Great. I'll hold you to that.' He took her hand and pressed it to his lips. 'I like you, Isla Milne. I like you a lot.'

'You're a nice guy too,' Isla told him, and then wished she hadn't because she didn't want to encourage him. She extracted her hand.

Presently, they left the shop, and after a quick look around The Pantiles, began to walk back up the hill towards the town, stopping periodically to window shop. They reached the top and encountered Jed Rowley waiting impatiently outside the old opera house. He raised his eyebrows when he saw them.

'I wondered where you'd got to, Dom. I thought we arranged to meet up around a quarter to.'

'Ah, well, that was before I ran into this fair maid. We've been for a coffee and a look around The Pantiles.'

'Right. Well, we'd best get a move on if we don't want to be late,' he said, rather tersely.

'Bye then, Isla — see you later.' Dom grinned and waved his hand.

Jed didn't say anything to her, and Isla felt distinctly embarrassed. Suddenly, she lost interest in the shopping she had planned to do and, after a cursory look round, picked up a few necessities and drove home. It was evident Jed thought she and Dom were going out together, and probably thought they'd planned to meet up all along, she thought miserably.

9

With just a few days left before the summer school began, Isla decided to visit her grandmother again. This time, she arranged to stay for lunch. Martha Milne was sitting in the garden chatting to a friend when she arrived.

'Hallo, love. This is my friend, Phyllis. We've known each other for donkeys' years.'

Isla chatted to the two elderly ladies until a carer turned up to take Phyllis for her physiotherapy session. Isla decided it was a golden opportunity for her to bring up the subject of Barns Cross. She told her grandmother of the visit to Rowley Grange and the conversation she'd had with Jerome and Jed Rowley regarding ancestors.

'Jerome Rowley mentioned that quite a few of his relatives used to live at Barns Cross at one time and seemed quite interested when I mentioned that the daughter of a friend of yours had married a Rowley.'

'Mmm. Did he actually tell you any of the first names of the relatives who'd lived at Barns Cross?'

'No — but Jed said he didn't know too much about his family tree.'

Gran made a noise which sounded suspiciously like a snort of disbelief.

'So, where exactly did this Jerome Rowley live before he came to Woodbridge?'

'Do you know, I haven't a clue. It didn't occur to me to ask that question. Jerome did seem quite interested in knowing how long we'd all lived there — particularly Ellen.'

Gran was silent for a moment. She knitted her fingers together and sat staring into space; then she said in a quiet voice, 'Ellen met her first husband in Barns Cross, when John brought him home for the holidays to stay with him.'

Isla stared at her. 'But I thought Uncle Tom was at Art College with

John and Aunt Ellen.'

'So he was, but he was also at grammar school with John before that, and that's how she first came to know him. She was swept away from the moment she clapped eyes on him.' She folded her arms. 'That's the way it was with that man. It's a wonder she ever finished her course, but mercifully she did.'

The carer was approaching, and Gran gathered her belongings together.

'Lunchtime. I must go and get ready. I'll see you in the dining-room in around fifteen minutes. Oh, and Isla, please don't mention what we've been talking about in front of Phyllis. She's a lovely soul but a bit of a sticky beak.'

She left Isla sitting on the seat, wondering why it would matter if she said anything in front of Phyllis. After all, it was hardly anything important. There was definitely something here that she didn't understand, but it looked like no-one was going to enlighten her.

* ⋆ ★

Isla was just preparing to leave when Gran called to her.

'I've suddenly remembered what that daughter of my friend, Hilda Platt was called. It was Irene. She was a very attractive young woman. There was a bit of scandal because Irene married one Rowley cousin and then, some years later, ran off with the other one.'

Isla's eyes widened. 'Goodness. No wonder Jerome Rowley didn't want to say much about them!'

Gran looked thoughtful. 'Did you say this Jerome Rowley was a widower?'

'I'm not sure. I've made friends with a girl called Amy Bradshaw. She might know.'

'Mm.' There was another story connected with Barns Cross, and Martha Milne just hoped that Isla didn't get to hear about it. She was usually discreet and was already beginning to regret saying anything at all to her granddaughter. It was best to let sleeping dogs lie, she decided, rather belatedly.

As usual, her grandmother had given her a lot of food for thought, Isla reflected as she wended her way home through the busy evening traffic. She wondered if Irene Platt was some relation — by marriage — of Jed's.

⋆   ⋆   ⋆

John's first summer school course was going with a swing. The students were a delightful bunch of beginners. John and Sam were introducing them to the basic techniques of pottery. They also gave several demonstrations of more advanced processes such as throwing, and one or two short lectures, accompanied by films of various archaeological discoveries during the ages to keep their interest alive and make them realise what they could aspire to.

After a morning's observation, Isla was happy to be more hands on. The students spent the first few sessions making first pinch and then coil pots. Jerome popped in periodically and on Thursday Jed appeared, just as John had gone to the workshop. Sam had gone home for the afternoon and Isla was sorting out a student's coil pot, which was sadly misshapen.

Wendy was very keen, but unfortunately had little aptitude for pottery. Isla was aware of Jed leaning over her shoulder, as she did her best to put things right and be encouraging to the middle-aged lady. Her heartbeat quickened and for a moment or two she was all fingers and thumbs. She pulled herself together with an effort. She got up and Wendy sat down again to make a valiant attempt with the pot.

Jed treated Isla to one of his charming smiles, sending a warm glow through her.

'Well done,' he said. Wendy, taking the praise to be for her, smiled back. He evidently had the ability to captivate the female population, Isla thought crossly.

At that stage, John reappeared laden

with materials, some of which slid to the floor. A couple of the students rushed to his rescue.

'I've just come by to remind everyone about Saturday evening. I hope you'll all be able to stay on. Fish and chips or a vegetarian option in the barn, and a get-together with the two groups before the new students arrive on Sunday.'

Most people said they were able to be there, and husbands, wives and partners were invited too. The other course that week, taken by Alice Mercer from the Arts Society, was on paper-cutting and sculpture. That group were involved in making cards and collages. Isla had been to have a look and she admired the delicate paper designs with their pastel colours. She was itching to have a go at it herself.

The two groups usually met up during coffee and tea breaks and at lunchtimes. Several of the ladies from the village helped out on these occasions, including Aunty June, who was obviously a much-loved character, and who regaled everyone with stories about the village.

After they had packed up for the day, Isla collected her things and began to walk back towards Ivy Cottage. It was a pleasant day and she had enjoyed herself immensely. John had stayed behind to sort out his work for the following day. She stopped off at the village shop to pick up a couple of items for Ellen and bumped into Amy Bradshaw.

'Hi there,' Amy greeted her. 'Dale's in London for yet another conference so I've been invited to Mum's for supper.'

They paid for their shopping and wandered back along the High Street together.

'So, how are things with you?' Amy wanted to know. 'Of course, it's the summer school this week. Is that going well?'

Isla filled her in with what she'd been up to since they'd last met, including meeting up with Dominic in Tunbridge Wells.

'Oh, yes, he said. Guess what?' she rushed on before Isla could say anything. 'Dale's taking me away for a mystery weekend in a week's time.' Her cheeks grew pink as she confided, 'It's my birthday and I'm wondering if he might pop the question. He's such a romantic soul, is Dale.'

Isla gave a little smile, hoping her friend wouldn't find out about Dale arranging for Dominic to sell the items of jewellery to the antique shop.

'Well, I hope the pair of you have a lovely time.' She suddenly remembered something. 'Amy, do you happen to know anything about Jerome Rowley's wife?'

Amy stared at her. 'Why would you ask that?'

'Oh, just curiosity. Jed never mentions his mother. Did she die?'

Amy wrinkled her brow. 'I'm not sure. If I remember I'll ask Mum. I don't ever recall seeing her in Woodbridge. As far as I remember, it's only ever been Jerome and Jed. You've made me curious now. I'll give you a ring if I discover anything, or you could ask Jed.'

'I don't think so. He comes across as quite a private person and I couldn't ask him a personal question like that.'

They had reached the turning to Ivy Cottage and, shortly afterwards, parted company. Isla knew she wouldn't get much response if she asked Ellen, apart from being told not to be inquisitive. Ellen was unlikely to be forthcoming; she was like a closed book when it suited her. Gran had often remarked that her two daughters had been like chalk and cheese. Isla's mother, Leona, had apparently been vivacious and full of fun, whereas Ellen had been the more serious one.

Ellen was in the kitchen making spaghetti Bolognese. For once, she was in a good mood. 'I'm going to be away this weekend. A friend of mine from Art College is visiting from France and staying in London. She wants a group of us to meet up. One of my other friends is putting me up for a couple of nights.'

'That'll be nice. What about John?' Isla asked, collecting cutlery from the drawer.

'Oh, he'll still be involved with the summer school, won't he? I expect they'll be having a social thing on Saturday and I'm not keen on those. Anyway, you'll be around to support him, won't you?'

'Yes, of course. I'm looking forward to it. They're a nice crowd.'

Ellen tasted the sauce and gave it another stir. 'Rather you than me. Those occasions bore me stiff, but of course it's all new to you, and John will be in his element. Now, did you remember to get parmesan cheese in the shop?'

Later that evening, Amy rang. 'I asked Mum about that thing you wanted to know about. She had no idea, but my grandmother was there, and she gave me the info. Apparently, Jerome was married to a woman called

Irene Platt. When Jed was in his teens, she upped and left them and went off to Scotland with Jerome's cousin.'

'Wow! That bears out what Gran said about her marrying one Rowley cousin and then going off with the other one! Jerome mentioned he'd had some relatives living in Barns Cross, but he didn't say anything about his wife having a liaison with his cousin!'

'Well, he wouldn't, would he?'

'I wonder if she's still alive.'

'Nan couldn't say, but Mum thought it was interesting. Other people's lives are, aren't they?'

'Sometimes. Thanks for filling me in. Enjoy your birthday if I don't see you before.'

'I will. We'll catch up when I get back. Have fun with the summer school.'

Isla sank down on the bed. She and Jed obviously had more in common than she'd realised. Her mother had died when she was twelve, and his had left him when he was not much older. It struck her as being odd that Jerome hadn't said anything about his ex-wife coming from Barns Cross when they had been talking about it. She supposed it must have been something he'd rather forget. She was curious to know where they had lived before they moved to Woodbridge.

One day when Ellen and John were safely in New Zealand, she decided, she would go to Barns Cross, and see if she could find the place where she herself had lived for the first two years of her life. Perhaps, she'd learn something about the Rowleys too.

★   ★   ★

All too soon, it was the end of the first summer school course. The students had finished the week with an introduction to decoration. They had made some tiles and used various objects to impress into the still-soft clay to make a pattern. John had provided them with some ready-made stamps produced from modelled clay coils. They were quite small and fiddly for beginners to make but using them gave them the idea of what they could achieve.

Some of them had chosen combing. For this, they had used old kitchen forks and plastic combs to cut parallel lines into the surface of the clay. They also had the opportunity to try their hand at decorating ready-made mugs and egg cups. They were pleased with the results.

The meal on Saturday was a great success. It seemed that, without exception, everyone had enjoyed themselves, and several had decided to enrol on the evening classes in the autumn and attend the additional Saturday course before then.

There was a small exhibition of the students' work in the barn, displayed on trestle tables and wall boards. It was amazing how much they had produced and there was a wide range of talent. John was going to fire some of the pottery, so the students would have the opportunity to collect it later, or he would arrange to pack it off to them.

After the meal, the chairs and tables were pushed to one side, and some of the students began to dance. To Isla's amusement, Jerome acted as DJ. John was a keen dancer and he whirled Isla round the floor a couple of times before she sank breathlessly onto a chair. She saw that Jed was gallantly dancing with Wendy and guessed from the older lady's face that that had made her day. Isla again realised what a thoughtful and caring person Jed was. A little later he came across to her and held out a hand.

'Care for a dance?' he asked softly. The music had slowed to a waltz for some of the more mature students. She allowed herself to be led onto the floor and felt a thrill run through her, as he put his hands on her waist and drew her close.

Her heartbeat quickened. 'You're looking lovely tonight,' he murmured against her cheek. His steps matched hers perfectly, and for a few minutes she was in a dream world where it was just the two of them twirling round to the strains of the music.

Her dream world was shattered by the alarm system blaring loudly. Jed caught her none-too-gently by the arm and bundled her out of the fire exit.

'Stay there,' he commanded, before disappearing inside again. After a few moments, he announced to the assembled crowd that all was well, and it was just an over-sensitive alarm system. The moment was passed and couldn't be recaptured.

Shortly afterwards the party broke up. Perhaps it was just as well, Isla told herself dully. She was becoming far too fond of Jed Rowley and sadly she had to accept that there was absolutely no future in it. Not while Nicole Trent was on the scene.

★   ★   ★

Isla ran into Jed again at church the following morning. She was talking to Penny after the service when he appeared. Isla could see John and Jerome; they were deep in discussion with one of the churchwardens. After a moment or two, Penny moved off.

'So, what are your plans for this afternoon?' Jed asked.

Isla stared at him in surprise. 'Well, I shall be at the Arts Centre at five o'clock for the meet and greet.'

'No, I meant before that. I was wondering if you fancied coming for a walk.'

She didn't want to appear too eager, even though her heart was beating so loudly that she felt sure he must hear it.

'Well, right now, I've got lunch to get for John because Ellen's away this weekend. He really fancies a shepherd's pie. An odd choice for a Sunday, but Ellen doesn't allow him to have it.'

Jed chuckled. 'I suspect Ellen has her own views on a healthy diet.'

Isla nodded. 'Mind you, John has hollow legs, so she does have to keep an eye on him — says it's for his own good.'

'But he's as lean as a bean — or do I mean as thin as a rake?'

It was Isla's turn to laugh. 'He's just one of those fortunate individuals who never seem to put on weight. Anyway, Ellen has her own agenda.'

'So, after that are you free? Unless, of course, you're planning to meet up with Dom?'

She ignored this. 'After that, I was planning to make a start on the painting for your father. I've done a few preliminary sketches and taken quantities of photos on my phone.'

'I know, we saw you from the window, but didn't like to disturb you. Anyway, I'm sure Dad isn't in any great hurry for the painting, and you do need a break so I thought perhaps we could take a walk to that special place I pointed out from the church tower a while back.'

Her face lit up. 'You mean the brook, and the bridge that is rumoured to have given Woodbridge its name? I'd really like that, Jed.'

'Then how about I meet you at the lychgate at around two thirty?'

'Yes, that would be great.'

John and Jerome arrived at that point and they parted company.

★   ★   ★

'That's the best shepherd's pie I've tasted in a long while,' John told her, taking a swig of beer out of the can. Ellen would have raised the roof!

After the apple crumble and cream she served for dessert, Isla left John to load the dishwasher whilst she dashed upstairs to make some running repairs to her appearance. Jed was already at the lychgate when she arrived.

As they set off, he asked, 'So are you planning to be as hands-on at the next course as you've been at this last one?'

'Even more so. The next lot of students are mainly from John's evening classes, so they're more advanced than this last group who were mostly beginners. I need to be acquainted with their level, because otherwise I'll be thrown in at the deep end when John departs for New Zealand in the middle of his final course. I could have wished they were also beginners, but if anything, they're more advanced than the next lot.'

'Well, not to worry. Sam will be there for most of the time, and if you get stuck, you can always call on me. I'll be around preparing for the course I'll be taking later in the month.'

Isla looked at him in surprise. 'Really? I didn't realise you were going to be taking a course. But your stuff is of such a high standard. I should think it would take months, even years, to get anywhere near that level.'

'Oh, you're too kind. Let me explain: the students in the courses I'll be taking are mainly drawn from folk I've been working with at my evening classes or at the Art College. Some of them are already teachers wanting to acquire an additional skill, but others just attend for pure enjoyment. And then there are my art students who are studying for their degrees and want to gain some extra experience. Anyway, I'm running these courses on making metal-clay jewellery.'

'It sounds fascinating.'

'It is. It's a relatively new medium and I love experimenting.'

They had skirted the boundary of the manor and were walking beyond the stables. Jed produced a key from his pocket and unlocked a gate almost concealed in a red brick wall. It led into a meadow strewn with wildflowers: poppies, cornflowers and oxeye daisies amongst them.

'Oh, how lovely,' she breathed, eyes shining.

'I thought you'd like it. We've left it as a wild patch; it attracts butterflies and a variety of other insects and wildlife. See, we've even got the common spotted-orchid. Now, there's a path near the hedge and that will lead down to the brook. It's a bit overgrown in places, so watch out for the brambles. In the autumn there are a mass of blackberries.'

She looked about her with pleasure. There were dog-roses in the hedgerow and wild mallow and cow parsley in the grass beneath, besides several flowers she couldn't name.

'It's my special secret place,' Jed confided. 'I don't bring many people here, but I suspected you would appreciate it.'

'Your suspicions were right — it's absolutely gorgeous. Thank you so much.'

He looked at her face, alight with enthusiasm, and knew that he wouldn't have got the same reaction from Nicole. He had never shown her this place because she wouldn't see it through his eyes as Isla had done.

Soon the path narrowed and led through a small beech copse down to the brook. Isla drank in every detail. They walked along the bank listening to birdsong and suddenly they came to the little bridge.

'Oh, wow!' Isla exclaimed. 'It's just so unexpected. Where does it lead?'

Jed knew he was taking a chance, but he so wanted her to see what was on the other side, and surely it could do no harm? So few people knew of its existence nowadays — apart from Sam Westfield, and probably Ellen.

He reached out a hand. 'Come, I'll show you. It's a bit narrow, but it's perfectly safe. The contact of his hand with hers and his body so close to her sent shivers trembling along her spine. She wondered if he'd ever brought Nicole here, although she couldn't imagine her being moved by it, if her reaction in the churchyard was anything to go by.

They looked over the bridge at the water swirling gently below, dark and mysterious.

'Sometimes there are water voles,' he told her. 'There are often moorhens, mallard ducks and a pair of egrets and, once or twice, I've caught sight of a kingfisher.'

They crossed the bridge and began to climb up a path towards a patch of trees. Suddenly, she stared in amazement; there in front of her was a green chalet.

'Did you put this here?' she wanted to know.

He shook his head. 'No. It was one of the reasons why I persuaded my father to purchase the land. It used to belong to an artist — Sam's cousin, actually. He was called Tom Westfield.'

10

Isla stared at him. 'Tom Westfield,' she repeated slowly, 'but he was my uncle at one time. He used to be married to my Aunt Ellen,'

Jed nodded. 'Yes, I know. John and Sam have both mentioned it.'

'So has my aunt ever been here?' she wanted to know.

'I suppose she must have done, years back, but not since she's lived here. She couldn't get here nowadays, you see, without our permission, and she's never approached us.'

He saw the stunned look on her face. 'Perhaps I was wrong to bring you here and, if so, I'm sorry.'

She put out a hand and touched his shoulder. 'No, Jed, don't be. It's such a lovely spot. I liked Uncle Tom, but I know he was a bit of a philanderer. Aunt Ellen is better off with John. But that doesn't prevent me from remembering Tom with affection, does it?'

'No, it certainly doesn't. Would you like to see inside? It's been repainted. Sometimes when I want to be by myself, I come down here to read or sketch.'

He unlocked the chalet and they went inside. She looked around in amazement. It had been set up like a small studio.

'I had no idea this existed. No-one has ever mentioned it. So, was this where Tom did his painting?'

Jed nodded. 'His father, Sam's uncle, worked at the manor as a gamekeeper and the owner recognised Tom's potential. Actually, he helped fund him when he went to Art College. He allowed him to use the chalet for his painting,'

'Wow I didn't know any of this! I don't suppose you ever got to meet Tom?'

'Several times, actually. I'm a few years older than you. I first met him when he came to Barns Cross to stay with John one summer.'

She looked at him in astonishment. 'Are you telling me that you lived at Barns Cross too?'

'Well, yes, I thought you knew. It's no big secret.'

'I suppose it didn't occur to me to ask where you lived before you came to Woodbridge. You didn't let on when I asked if you'd got any relatives living there.'

'Because I thought you knew already,' he repeated.

'Well, life's full of surprises — that's two I've had this afternoon. You know, I've an idea I've seen an unframed painting of this place somewhere, I can't quite remember. I suppose it might have been when we were turning out Gran's house. Aunt Ellen got rid of a lot of stuff, but I can't imagine John letting that go. I'll ask him.'

'I hope he won't mind my bringing you here,' Jed said.

'I don't see why he should. After all, Tom died years back and I think it's great that you've kept his memory alive by restoring the chalet,'

Jed was giving her a strange look. 'What? I didn't realise Tom had died. When was this?'

'I was in my teens — around fifteen. He had a heart attack.'

For a moment, Jed didn't reply. Then, he said slowly, 'Isla, according to your CV, you're rather more than twenty-one.'

She was puzzled by this comment. 'You know I am. I'm almost thirty. Why?'

'Because it was only around six years ago when I last saw Tom Westfield. Yes, he'd had a heart attack, but that was way back and he was doing very well.'

Isla had gone pale. 'Where did you see him?' she demanded.

'Here; he came here one summer, just as he used to all those years ago. And I can assure you that he was very much alive. Someone's told you wrongly.'

Isla sank onto a bench. 'I don't understand — why would they tell me such a story?'

'I can't imagine. And they've gone on

allowing you to believe it.' He sat down beside her and put a comforting arm about her shoulder. For a moment, she didn't trust herself to speak. She leant against him and stared into space for a moment or two.

'So, where does Tom live now?'

'Oh, he's abroad somewhere — Canada, I think. He'll pop up again at some point. I'm sorry you've had such a shock, Isla.'

'It's good to know Uncle Tom is still alive, but I can't imagine why everyone wanted me to believe he was dead,' she said bleakly. 'I honestly believe Ellen is a lot happier with John. She's said so herself.'

Privately, Jed was unable to process the information he'd just been given. He'd deliberately steered clear of mentioning Tom to Isla on the advice of Sam, understanding that it was a taboo subject where Ellen and John were concerned, but he'd no idea Isla thought Tom had died. He could only assume that it was Ellen's way of dealing with things — pretending that Tom was no longer around.

He put his backpack on the wooden table. There's no electricity of course, but there's a small camping stove here and I've brought everything we need, including bottled water, for a cup of builder's tea, which I think we could both do with.'

'I don't understand why Uncle Tom hasn't been in touch,' she said, as they sat with mugs of tea presently. 'He was a lovely guy. I understand that Ellen wouldn't have wanted him around, but she didn't live with my grandparents and me, and once she'd married John then surely there was no harm.'

'Perhaps there was more to the story than you were aware of, and it was their way of making sure you didn't keep in touch.'

She nodded. 'Yes, I suppose that has to be it. The problem is, I can't ask Ellen. She will very rarely open up about the past. Perhaps I'll speak to John, although I'm frankly amazed that they haven't kept in touch if they were the good friends you indicated.'

Jed was amazed too. They drank tea and munched the cherry flapjacks Gemma had made.

'I'm not a child, and I wish they wouldn't treat me like one. If Tom is alive then it's up to me if I want to keep in touch with him, isn't it?'

Isla looked so forlorn that he slung his arm around her again and drew her close. She felt warm and secure in his arms. Everything seemed topsy-turvy at the moment, but somehow this seemed right. Before she knew it, he was kissing her, gently at first and then, when she didn't object, becoming more impassioned. She reached up and entangled her fingers in his hair. He stroked her face, kissed her throat. Emotions engulfed her and their kisses deepened. Eventually, he pulled away.

'I'm sorry Isla — I didn't intend . . .'

She smiled shakily. 'Don't be. This place has its own particular brand of magic, doesn't it?'

'Yes, indeed it does.' He swept up the cups and wiped them with kitchen paper before returning them to his backpack. She popped the rest of the debris into the container, pressed on the lid and handed it to him.

They walked back to the Grange practically in silence, each immersed in their own thoughts. Isla knew that their relationship had changed back there in the chalet and that things would never be the same between them again, even though she knew that there was no future in it. She knew that Nicole was there in the background, and that sadly she would just have to accept that. A few stolen kisses weren't going to change anything — however much Isla might wish it.

★   ★   ★

Isla believed there was no time like the present. Ellen wasn't due to return until Monday morning and so after the meet and greet at the Arts Centre, and the short get-together, she tackled John over supper.

'John, why has everyone pretended all of these years that Tom Westfield died from that heart attack?'

John's head shot up. 'Has Sam been talking to you about Tom? I distinctly asked him not to.'

'No, John, it wasn't Sam, but you must have realised that sooner or later I was going to find out. All I want to know is: why?'

He shook his head. 'It was your grandfather and Ellen. She wanted to make a fresh start and your grandfather was upset at the way Tom had treated her. We thought it was for the best to sever all contact.'

'Well, it was a pretty drastic way to do it by pretending that he'd died. After all, from what I understand, he's abroad now so he was hardly likely to hang around and make a nuisance of himself, was he now? I was fond of Uncle Tom and I thought he was your best friend.'

'Isla, you are old enough to understand now, but then you were just fifteen. Younger than that, when Tom and Ellen parted company. There are things you don't know about Tom. I'd known Ellen for years and we were going out together when we were still at school, but from the moment Tom clapped eyes on her that all ended. That was how it's always been with Tom. He seemed to have a magnetic quality where women were concerned. Unfortunately, he didn't have the commitment needed in a strong relationship and marriage, and things didn't work out.

'Ellen was always the girl for me. I was heartbroken when she chose Tom, but I wanted her to be happy and couldn't bear to learn how he'd treated her. When things didn't work out, I was around to pick up the pieces. It was a long wait, but worthwhile.'

This was a long speech for John. 'Were you afraid that Tom might come back to Ellen? Was that why you decided he had to stay away?'

213

'When Ellen makes up her mind there's no changing it. You should know that. She's very like her father in that respect. It would have been difficult for Tom and me to remain friends in the circumstances. Your grandfather had never liked him and was furious with him for the way he behaved. You kept asking about him and why you weren't allowed to see him. I realise you missed him, and so when he had the heart attack, it was a golden opportunity for us to finally close the chapter and tell you that he had died.'

'It was cruel and wicked,' she burst out. 'He was always kind to me and to make out he had died when he hadn't — that's despicable!'

John looked shamefaced. 'You're right, it was. It wasn't my idea, Isla — or your grandmother's.'

'But you went along with it. All these years I've believed he was dead.' She set her knife and fork down, her appetite gone. 'I thought better of you, John. I don't even know how to contact him, or

I can assure you I would.'

'Sam might know.' John ventured.

'Well, you've obviously told him to let me go on believing that Tom had died. What sort of fool do you think that makes me feel? Apparently, everyone knows the truth except for me.'

Isla crossed to the sink and filled the kettle, blinking back the tears.

'Isla, I'm so sorry. I told Ellen it was a bad idea at the time. But now we've moved on and she rarely mentions Tom.'

'You might have moved on, but I haven't. Oh, don't worry; I shan't say anything to Ellen. This conversation can stay strictly between the two of us, although I might mention it to Gran.'

John looked horrified. 'Isla, please don't say anything about this to your grandmother. She's frail and there's no point upsetting her. Raking up the past is never a good idea. Let's put it to rest, eh?'

'It's all very well for you, John. You know what really happened. For me,

I've only just discovered the truth. I've got to come to terms with it. Tom is a part of my past too, remember.'

John gave a little shrug. 'No good can come of raking things up, Isla. Now, there's a good documentary on TV, so how about we take our pudding into the living-room together with a nice cup of tea and watch it?'

John was all for a quiet life, Isla decided, as she made the tea. He was very good at burying his head in the sand and ignoring the situation. Well, she would just have to wait until he and Ellen had gone to New Zealand, and then do a little family research in Barns Cross.

* * *

The students on John's second course were far more advanced than on the previous one. Some of them had been to his evening classes and wanted to finish work they'd already begun. Others wanted to learn new techniques or work on their own projects, and several were studying at Art College, and wanted to add to their skills.

Isla was just about one jump ahead of them and becoming increasingly concerned that they might suss this out.

She had decided to take Wednesday off to visit Gran, but Sam rang on Tuesday evening to say that Mollie was not at all well, and he'd need to take the day off.

'I could manage on my own, but it's always useful to have an extra pair of hands,' John told her apologetically.

Most of the students were happy to get on with their work. John had given out detailed notes on various techniques. He had demonstrated several of these and shown them one or two short films. Just before break, he had gone over to the kiln room, leaving Isla temporarily in charge. She walked round, offering advice and helping out when called upon.

Several of the students had already made their pottery in John's previous classes and had brought their pieces back to get them biscuit-fired, ready to be glazed on this course. Others were trying out various forms of decoration. Zena, a talented but temperamental young woman, looked up impatiently as Isla approached.

'Could you ask Faye to be more careful when she's using that spray gun? She's getting slip all over the place,' she complained, as she skilfully applied a cutaway sponge to stamp a pattern onto her biscuit-fired milk jug. She was one of John's college students and made it clear that she didn't suffer fools gladly.

'Why don't you ask her yourself?' Isla asked her. 'Those guns can have a mind of their own, but I'm sure she's not being deliberately annoying.'

Isla was aware of several pairs of eyes, watching and waiting. Everyone knew that Zena had an elevated opinion of herself and was a troublemaker.

'Oh, I might have known you'd take her side; although why I should take any notice of you, I wouldn't know.

After all, you're not in charge. Anyway, where's Sam today?'

'We did explain at the beginning of the session that as his wife was ill, and that I'd be stepping in,' Isla said patiently.

'You were late coming over, Zena,' one of the other students pointed out.

'That's a beautiful design, Faye,' another remarked, obviously trying to diffuse the situation.

There was silence for a few moments as everyone concentrated on what they were doing. Suddenly, there was another outburst from Zena.

'Faye, you've just spattered slip all over me. You really are a pain in the neck!'

Faye, a nervous lady, apologised profusely and burst into tears just as the door opened to admit Jed. He summed the situation up in a couple of minutes.

'Now, ladies. I'm sure it was an accident. Shall we all take five — unless you're in the midst of a delicate procedure. There's some wonderful work going on here and we don't want to risk spoiling it.'

'Then you'd better tell her that,' Zena said pointedly, looking at Isla, who coloured. Faye went out of the room and one of the other students followed her. Isla wished she could join them.

'Where's John?' Jed asked.

Isla explained and he nodded and said in a low tone, 'Well, just try to keep a lid on it for a few more minutes, and we'll take an early coffee break. Don't look so worried, Isla. I've had my fair share of artistic temperaments, believe you me.'

During the coffee break, John said, 'Zena isn't the easiest of students, Isla. She's been spoilt rotten and pampered by over-indulgent rich parents. She is one of the students who kicked up a fuss when she discovered I'm not able to complete my third course, which is why she's been transferred to this one.'

'Well, that's some small comfort, I suppose. Seriously, John, I just hope I can manage to cope with everything whilst you're away. The standard is pretty high, and I hadn't anticipated it being quite at this level.'

'Oh, you'll be fine,' John reassured her. 'Anyway, I'm sure Sam will be there, and he'll be overall in charge. If it's any consolation, Zena may think she's brilliant, but her work isn't original. She's actually purloined that design from a photograph. If you notice, she's copying it quite cleverly.'

Isla's eyes widened. 'Really? Oh, that does make me feel better.'

'Not only that, but in spite of what she's making out, that technique is really not that difficult once you've mastered it. Some of the other students are doing things that are far more complicated.'

Fortunately, the day passed with no further incidents and on Thursday Sam returned, saying that Mollie was much better, and so Isla was able to make a quick visit to Bexhill.

When Isla arrived, she found her grandmother sitting in the conservatory staring into space. She was delighted to see her granddaughter.

'Phyllis has gone out to lunch with her son and I thought I was going to die of boredom,' she complained. 'It's too chilly to sit in the garden today and it's been drizzling. So, tell me what you've been up to.'

Isla was tempted to come straight out with what she'd discovered about Tom Westfield but remembered her promise to John. She did, however, drop one or two leading remarks into the conversation to see her grandmother's reaction.

'So, the Rowleys at the Grange in Woodbridge used to live in Barns Cross. Well, well!' Gran mused. 'Of course, I'd forgotten that all the eldest sons were called Jerome, so I suspect that the Jerome who lives at Woodbridge Grange now *is* the one that was married to Irene Platt.'

'I would think so. I gather that she went off with Jerome's cousin and lives in Scotland now.'

Gran sniffed. 'Well, she always was no better than she ought to be — flighty piece'

'Would you remember Jed Rowley from when he was a little boy?' Isla asked curiously, as the thought suddenly struck her.

'Oh, yes. Now I know who you're talking about, love. I saw him in church on occasion or at village functions, but our paths didn't cross that much because he lived at the opposite end of the village from us in a big house up on the hill. Anyway, we didn't mix in the Rowley's circles. Now, I come to think of it, I remember that Irene Platt wasn't a very good mother. The little lad seemed to spend a lot of time with his grandparents, both at Barns Cross and at the Grange in Woodbridge. Hilda, Irene's mother, once told me that Irene wasn't the maternal type. She was always gadding about, and the little lad was an encumbrance.'

'Poor Jed! Everyone seems to be connected to everyone else. I know that Sam Westfield, who works with John, is Tom's cousin.'

She had steered the conversation

carefully round to the subject she really wanted to discuss with her grandmother.

Her grandmother leaned forward on her chair. 'And so he might be. Isla, don't go rooting about in the past. We've all moved on now. Your Aunt Ellen and Uncle John are happy, and it's best to leave things be.'

'That's all very well, but now that I'm living so near to Barns Cross, where I spent the first two years of my life, I'm obviously curious about it. Anyway, whatever you might think of Uncle Tom, he obviously had a good influence on Jed Rowley.'

'Oh, how do you make that one out?' She fixed Isla with an intense look from her bright blue eyes.

'Jed is a very fine artist. He's a sculptor actually — bronze and clay. He's very talented and he told me it was Uncle Tom who encouraged his interest in art.'

Gran was pleating the material of her skirt restlessly. 'Oh, I wouldn't know about that. I suppose he must have had some good points. He encouraged you to paint, too.'

'Yes, he did. He bought me my first paint-box and set of brushes.'

Gran laughed. 'I've still got one of the first paintings you ever did. It was supposed to have been of your grandfather. Ellen didn't quite manage to get me to throw away *everything*.'

Isla laughed too and then gave her grandmother a searching look. 'Gran, I know this is a difficult question, but have you really got no idea of who my father was?'

Gran gave a deep sigh. 'We've had this conversation before, over the years. I wish you would let it rest, love. It doesn't do to speculate.'

'Well, it hardly matters if you tell me now, Gran. What harm can it do?'

There was a set look on Martha Milne's face that Isla knew only too well. She could tell that, even if the elderly lady did have any idea, she also had no intention of divulging anything.

Isla knew from experience that it would be like getting blood out of a stone.

There was a silence before Gran said, 'I implore you, Isla, to leave the subject well alone. Now here's Mary, come to get me ready for lunch. Shall I see if we can squeeze you in?'

Isla stayed to lunch with her grandmother, then dropped in on her friends, Kate and Matt, and spent a pleasant couple of hours before collecting more of her possessions from their garage and driving home. She was more convinced than ever that her grandmother knew the identity of her father and felt frustrated that the old lady chose to keep her in the dark.

11

Isla was quite relieved when the second week of the summer school drew to a close. She had found it challenging and hadn't enjoyed it as much as the first week. Surprisingly, the students declared they'd had a wonderful time and were pleased with what they had achieved. They told John and Sam they couldn't wait to continue with their classes in September. Even Zena seemed to have enjoyed herself and had quietened down. They had certainly produced a wonderful display of work for the exhibition on Saturday.

'Sam, I do hope you don't mind my being foisted upon you when John goes off to New Zealand,' Isla said anxiously.

'Oh, we'll make a great team,' he assured her, his brown eyes twinkling. 'You've really fitted in and I'm looking forward to working alongside you.'

'Jed took me to see Tom's chalet last weekend,' she said quietly.

Sam raised his eyebrows. 'Did he now? Then you are privileged — he doesn't let many people go there.'

'Why did you let me go on believing that Tom had died?'

Sam looked taken aback. 'I was in an awkward position, Isla. John had filled me in with what the family had told you all those years back. I didn't ask any questions, just respected their decision. I understood it was for Ellen's sake.'

'Are you still in touch with him?' she asked.

Sam stroked his beard and looked even more awkward. 'Only at Christmas. I suppose it was Jed who mentioned that Tom's still very much alive and living abroad?'

'Of course. He was astounded when he discovered I thought Tom had died.' She sighed. 'Oh, I don't blame you, Sam, you were just doing what you thought was right.'

'Families, eh?' he said.

Isla pulled a face. 'Yes, they can be a headache sometimes . . . Now, we still need to find a space for these two vases.'

★ ★ ★

That weekend was different from the previous one. Jed didn't put in an appearance on Saturday evening until the meal was almost over and seemed in a sombre mood. Isla wondered if it had anything to do with Nicole. He can't have had much time to spend with her recently. Fortunately, there was a week before John's final course began, and so everyone could have a breathing space. Isla planned to get on with her painting of Rowley Grange for Jerome Rowley.

Jerome came to sit beside her now. 'Well, that's another successful week, Isla. The standard is quite amazing.'

'Yes, John and Sam can be really proud of themselves,' Isla said.

'And you, my dear. I know that

you've filled in for Sam and your contributions haven't gone unnoticed.'

She coloured. 'I've really enjoyed helping out and it's given me a good insight into how John runs his classes. I'm feeling more confident about assisting Sam when John goes to New Zealand now.'

'Oh, I'm sure you will cope admirably.'

'I'm hoping to make a beginning on your painting of Rowley Grange next week, if that's OK with you?'

'Wonderful. If you need anything just go around to the side door and through to the kitchen. It's always open when Gemma's around during the daytime.'

★ ★ ★

Isla was thwarted in her attempt at making a start on the painting, however. Ellen was getting increasingly anxious about the number of things she needed to do before her holiday and was delegating some of them to her niece.

It was Wednesday afternoon before Isla finally got to Rowley Grange. She set up her easel at the front of the house and had been working for about an hour and a half when Jed's Ferrari shot up the drive. A moment or two later, he appeared by her side. Her heartbeat quickened.

'Wow! I can see you've made a good start. I like what I'm seeing,' he informed her, standing several paces back, his head on one side. 'Now, I'm desperate for a cup of tea; are you ready to take a break?'

'Actually, yes, that would be lovely.' She stood up and popped the brushes into the pot of water on the ledge.

'Did Dad tell you where you could wash your brushes?'

'Actually, he wasn't around, but I found an outside tap.'

'Oh, we can do better than that.' He slung an arm about her shoulder and walked her round the side of the house and in through a small door to a passageway.

'Should you need to wash and brush up, the facilities are through that door, and to your left is what we call the flower room — ideal for washing paint brushes. Oh, and always feel free to make yourself a coffee if no-one's around. The kitchen's just along here.'

It was a huge kitchen; despite its modern appliances, it was somehow still in character. The units were in green and cream and there was a wonderful butler's sink and a range.

She looked down at her paint-spattered shirt. 'I'm not exactly dressed for taking tea in your lovely sitting-room.'

He grinned. 'Dad's out today so I thought we'd have tea in the conservatory at the back of the house. Dad finds it a bit hot this time of the year and prefers the sitting-room.'

Excusing herself, she went to make use of the rather old-fashioned facilities he'd pointed out as they'd come in. She splashed water on her face and attempted to tidy her hair, but strands kept escaping from the scrunchie she'd secured it with, so in the end she gave up. When she returned, he was laying a tea-tray.

'Gemma's made a fresh batch of treacle scones, my all-time favourite, and there is banana tea bread with butter.'

The conservatory was enormous and full of hothouse plants. They sat facing the garden and Jed switched the fan on. Tabby came to join them, purring loudly.

Tea was delicious and she savoured every mouthful. Ellen wasn't into eating between meals, so this was a treat.

'John and Ellen are going away next week?'

Isla nodded and finished her mouthful. 'John will be in for the first three days of his course, and then we'll be taking over. It will be quite a challenge.'

'And one that you'll rise to, I feel sure.'

'I'll do my best,' she assured him. 'Jed, I tried speaking to Gran about

Tom, but I didn't get anywhere. She clams up whenever I approach the subject,' she said presently. 'I've also mentioned it to Sam, because I couldn't understand why he let me go on thinking that Tom had died.'

Jed put down his piece of tea bread and surveyed her, 'Oh, and what did *he* say?'

'Just that everyone thought it was for the best that way. Apparently, as I'd suspected, John had had a word with him. Anyway, I've decided to take a look at Barns Cross when John and Ellen are in New Zealand.'

'Really? Then, if you like, I'll come with you. I haven't been there for quite a number of years. It's one of those rambling sorts of villages. We used to live on the west side — up on the hill.'

'Then I suppose my grandparents' house was on the east side?'

'I expect so. So, what's made you suddenly become so curious about where you first lived?'

Isla considered. 'Oh, I think selling

up Gran's house made me feel a bit restless. It was as if suddenly I didn't belong anywhere anymore, so I thought I'd like to do a bit of family research — find my roots.'

'There's nothing wrong in that. Now, would you like another slice of tea bread?'

'I shouldn't, but it's too delicious to refuse. I expect you've got a really interesting family history, Jed.'

'What?' The knife suspended in mid-air as he swung round to face her, the glint back in his eyes. 'What makes you say that?'

'I meant because of the past generations of Rowleys.'

'Oh, yes, I see. Probably, although I haven't looked into it too much. I never seem to have the time.'

He cut the tea bread and passed it to her. She buttered it absently. His reaction had surprised her, but then she remembered what she'd been told about Irene Platt, his mother. Isla knew that she would hate questions about her father; in her case, because she knew absolutely nothing about him — not even his name. Possibly, Jed felt the same about his mother, but for a different reason.

After tea, he said, 'How about a stroll round my father's prize rose garden?'

'That would be lovely, Jed, but at this rate I'm not going to get very far with your father's painting.'

'Oh, there's no rush, and you've made a good start,' he said, and catching her by the hand, led her into the garden across the lawn and through a small gate. She caught her breath. The rose garden was stunning, with blooms of every hue and colour.

'It was my grandfather's pride and joy at one time. He had a wonderful gardener of around the same age as himself, but as they grew older it got a bit much for the pair of them and became neglected. They died within months of each other. Dad has worked on it with the help of a younger chap, and it's gradually been transformed to its former glory. You can see the result.'

The fragrance was heady, and she sniffed appreciatively. Wherever she looked there was a profusion of roses scrambling up walls and rambling over pergolas and arbours. In the centre was a circular paved area with a small sun dial.

'It's absolutely beautiful,' she told him, pausing to examine a white rose that was flowering in abundance nearby. The outer edges of its petals were tinged with pink. Nearby was an arbour with a seat beneath. Small pink roses cascaded all around. Suddenly she was in his arms, and he was kissing her as if he never meant to stop, and she responded with all her heart.

'You are beautiful too,' he told her softly against her hair. She reached up and entwined her hands about his neck. For a few moments they were lost in their own world. It was as if she was in a wonderful dream, and she could have stayed in his arms for ever.

Eventually, they sank onto the seat

and sat in silence for a few moments. Bees hummed busily in the roses; the scent was intoxicating. Reluctantly, and with a sigh, she got to her feet.

'You've shown me another painters' paradise,' she told him. 'I could stay here for ever, but I ought to do a little more work on my own painting.'

As they crossed the hall, Dominic Irwin came out of the office. 'I wondered where you'd got to, Jed. There are some letters I need you to sign, and a few things I need to run past you.' His gaze turned to Isla. 'Pleased I've bumped into you, Isla. How about us meeting up for lunch, before you get tied up with the next course? Would Friday suit you?'

'I — um — I'm not sure. I'll give you a ring,' she told him, aware that Jed had stiffened. The two men disappeared into the office and she went across the front lawn to her easel. She couldn't concentrate and wished Dom hadn't appeared at that precise moment. It had been so idyllic in the rose garden. She remembered Jed's kisses and smiled. For a few moments she'd allowed herself to be transported to a place where dreams come true, but now she was back in the real world.

A smart white sports car zoomed up the drive and came to a stop. Nicole elegantly stepped out, and catching sight of Isla, came across.

'Have you seen Jed?' she asked, flicking back her hair.

'Yes, he's talking with Dominic in the office.'

She came closer. 'Did you know you've got rose petals in your hair?'

'Oh, that's because I've been walking round the garden.' Isla reached up and brushed them off.

'Really. So, what exactly are you doing here?'

'Jerome Rowley has asked me to paint a picture of the Grange.'

Nicole came across and looked. She reached out a finger and deliberately touched the painting, smudging it in a couple of places.

'Oh, dear, it's still wet.' She made a great thing of finding a tissue and wiping her fingers. 'Paint is such a messy medium, isn't it,' she said, eyeing Isla's paint-stained shirt.

Jed had seen Nicole from the window and came out of the front door, taking the steps in rapid strides.

'Hallo, Nicole. I wasn't expecting to see you today.'

'Thought I'd surprise you, darling.' She went across to him and lifted her face up to be kissed. 'If Jerome wanted a picture of the house, then why on earth didn't you paint him one yourself?'

'Because my father asked Isla,' he told her rather curtly.

'Yes, I realise that, but when he's got an artist living on the premises . . . Oh, I see. Isla needs the money and your father, out of the kindness of his heart — '

Isla flushed scarlet, and Jed took Nicole firmly by the arm and led her indoors. To top it all, it began to rain without any warning. Isla snatched up her easel, but the damage was done. She could have burst into tears when she looked at the ruined painting. The afternoon that had started so full of promise had ended up being a disaster.

★   ★   ★

Amy rang up that evening, asking Isla to join her and Dale for lunch on Friday.

'I'm not sure if Dom's spoken to you yet.'

A surge of relief swept through Isla as she realised Dominic wasn't asking her to an intimate lunch for two.

'Briefly, this afternoon at the Grange. I didn't realise it was to be all four of us.'

'Would you rather it wasn't?' Amy asked, in a teasing tone.

'No, no of course not, but Dom made it sound like that — and Jed was there.'

'Well, that's Dom for you. It's only fish and chips at that restaurant on the main road. I haven't caught up with you since my weekend away.'

'Oh, I meant to ring you to find out if your weekend away met up to your expectations.'

Amy giggled. 'You'll have to wait and see, won't you? Dale really pushed the boat out — took me to Prague. It was magical. So, I take it you'll be there around one o'clock?'

'Absolutely, but you'll have to explain to me exactly where it is.'

'Oh, I forget you're not a local yokel. Not to worry, one of us will pick you up at twelve thirty from Ivy Cottage.'

'I'll look forward to it,' Isla told her, relaxing now that she realised it was to be a group outing.

★   ★   ★

On Thursday afternoon, Isla returned to the Grange for a second attempt at the painting. This time things went well. She was pleased with what she'd achieved, deciding it was much better than the first time round. Perhaps it was just as well that Nicole had smudged the previous one.

To her relief, there was no sign of Jed or Dom, but just as she was packing up, Jerome Rowley appeared on the steps and waved.

'I didn't want to disturb you, but I'm itching to see how you're getting on.'

'Much better than yesterday. It was a disaster area.' She didn't mention Nicole, not wishing to make it sound as if she was blaming her. 'Just as I was about to pack away it began to rain. My painting was spoilt, and I've had to begin all over again. Today I've come armed with a sheet of polythene.'

'Oh, my dear, what bad luck! May I?' Jerome stood looking over her shoulder without uttering a word for so long that she wondered if he disliked what he saw.

'That's amazing,' he said at last. 'You've captured the house superbly.'

'It's far from finished, but it's much better than yesterday's effort,' she told him modestly. 'Unfortunately, I'm not going to have too much time to spare once the next summer school course starts.'

'You've been slaving away for what seems like hours. Would you like some refreshments?'

She was about to refuse when she saw his expectant expression. 'Only if we can have them out here,' she told him. 'I'm in no fit state to come into your beautiful sitting-room.'

'Then we'll have it on the terrace. Gemma's here this afternoon. I'll get her to bring tea outside.'

'I'll just go and tidy up,' Isla told him. A short while later, she joined him on the terrace. Tabitha was fast asleep on one of the garden seats. She tried not to think about the previous afternoon with Jed in the rose garden.

'Jed's out with Nicole,' Jerome volunteered. 'Some business luncheon up in London to do with her work. He's her plus one.'

'I understand she's very successful,'

Isla said generously.

Jerome was liberally applying cream to his scone. 'So she would lead us to believe. Have you managed to get to see your grandmother again?'

'I saw her at the end of last week, and I speak to her on the phone fairly regularly. She seems to have settled into the home very well, although she gets frustrated because she can't manage to do as much as she would like to do.'

'You know, I *can* remember your family from years back when they used to live in Barns Cross. Jed was talking to me about it the other day and it jogged my memory.'

'Yes, it's strange coming across people who knew them. I was only two years old when we moved to Bexhill and Ellen was married by that time.'

'Yes, to Sam's cousin, Tom. She was a good-looking girl — still is, for that matter. So was your mother, come to that. I wondered who you reminded me of, and then I realised: you're very like your mother, you know.'

'Yes, so I believe. I was only twelve when she died in a tragic accident.'

'It must have been hard for you,' he said sympathetically.

Isla sipped her tea. 'Yes, it was, but my grandparents were there for me. I don't know what I would have done without them.'

She hoped Jerome wasn't going to bring up the question of her father — unless, of course, he could throw some light on who he was. But Jerome didn't say any more and they sat in silence for a few moments, each immersed in their own thoughts.

'Jed tells me he took you to see the rose garden,' he said presently.

Her pulse raced as she remembered. 'Yes, it's very beautiful. There was one particular rose that I fell in love with, in the middle of the garden near that little sun dial. It was white with a slight tinge of pink on the outer petals. The fragrance was wonderful.'

Jerome looked pleased. 'That would be the Margaret Merril — I'm not sure who she was, but it's a magnificent floribunda and a firm favourite of mine. I'm glad you like it because, although it had to be replaced, my father planted the original one in memory of my mother.'

'Then he chose well,' she told him warmly.

'Yes, he did. When you've finished your painting of the house, perhaps you'd like to do one of the rose garden?'

Isla's face broke into a smile. 'I'd be delighted, Jerome. What I did want to do, however, was another view of the back of the Grange. That lends itself to a painting too. That would just be for my own pleasure, if you would let me. No payment needed.'

'My dear girl,' he began, but on seeing the determined look on her face, he simply said, 'Well, we'll see when the time comes. Now, how about another cup of tea?'

★ ★ ★

Dominic turned up at Ivy Cottage to take Isla to lunch the following day. He was wearing a checked shirt and jeans. He exchanged a few words with Ellen and, catching hold of Isla's arm, led her away to his car.

'It seems ages since we last met up,' he said as they sped away.

'That's because it is. I've been busy with the summer school and I expect you've been kept occupied too.'

'Oh, there's always plenty to do, but Jed's out of the office and won't be back until late afternoon, so as I've tied up most of the loose ends, I feel justified in taking a few hours off. Jerome has sanctioned it. So, how's the painting coming along?'

'Oh, it's taking shape, but it's early days. It'll need many more hours than I've got spare at the moment. As I expect you're aware, John and Ellen are off to New Zealand next week and I'm assisting Sam for the rest of the course.'

'Yes, I had heard that. I also heard

that the previous group were a bit of a handful.'

'Oh, they weren't that bad — just a bit of artistic temperament,' she said generously. 'So, changing the subject, I take it that selling the jewellery proved worthwhile?'

'If you mean my brother's weekend away, then yes — but I'm sure Amy wants to tell you herself, so you'll need to be patient for a tad longer.'

Presently, they pulled up in the car park of the fish restaurant. Amy and Dale were already there, and it only took a couple of minutes for Isla to spot the solitaire diamond ring on Amy's engagement finger.

After the congratulations, Amy and Dale enthused about Prague until Dom raised his hand in protest. 'Enough. You two sound like an advert for a travel programme. Perhaps Isla and I should sample the delights for ourselves. How about it, Isla?'

Isla's cheeks burned as she saw the gleam in his eyes. 'In your dreams,

Dom. I'll be tied up in Woodbridge for weeks to come.'

'Pity — I might have to find myself another girl then,' he said, eyes dancing with merriment.

Fortunately, the waitress appeared to take their order just then. Looking at Amy, her eyes sparkling as brightly as the diamond in her ring, Isla felt a sharp pang of envy. Happiness like that seemed to have eluded her. She knew now, without a shadow of doubt, that things would never have worked out between herself and Ewan. As for Dom: he was good company, but definitely not her type.

She thought of Jed. If only he was not involved with Nicole. There was an ache inside her. The feel of his lips on hers had awakened every fibre in her being. She realised she was in danger of falling in love with him.

The fish meal was tasty and Isla found herself relaxing. They were a fun set of youngsters and she knew she was lucky to have them as friends. It was almost four o'clock by the time Dom drove her back to Woodbridge. He told her he had to go back to the Grange to do a bit of work.

'I really enjoy your company, Isla,' he told her as he pulled up in the lane. 'Perhaps next time we can go out together as just the two of us. Oh, darn there's someone behind me. Well, he'll just have to wait!'

Taking her unawares, he leant across and kissed her hard on the mouth. Isla pulled away. 'Dom, when will you ever take *no* for an answer — that was . . . '

'Nice?' he suggested, grinning infuriatingly.

As she got out of the car, she realised the driver in the car behind, waiting impatiently at the wheel, was Jed, and realised Dominic must have known that before he kissed her. Her cheeks flamed and she wished with all her heart that it hadn't been Jed. He must have witnessed that kiss and would now get completely the wrong impression of her relationship with Dominic Irwin.

12

On Saturday evening, John sought Isla out. Ellen was busy sorting out her clothes for the impending trip.

'I keep telling her jeans and shirts will be the order of the day for most of the trip, but the evenings can be chilly, so she'll need some woollies too. After all, it's approaching winter over there.

'Now Isla, we're arranging for some money to go into your banking account for the general housekeeping, general expenses for Gran, et cetera. As you know, Gran's fees and our domestic bills are all set up by direct debit, so no worries on that score. Anyway, you can always e-mail me over any problems.'

'Yes, Ellen's already explained all that,' she said, wondering what he was driving at.

John produced an envelope. 'This is some extra cash for you, Isla. You've been wonderful in helping out with the art projects and summer school courses. You've been a real asset and it's time you had some money to spend on yourself.'

'Oh, that's really not necessary, John. I've enjoyed what I've been doing. I've sold a few paintings and Jerome is going to pay me for the one I'm doing of the Grange so I'm hardly penniless,' she protested.

'And Jed will see to it that you get paid for the work you're putting in next week when you help to run the course. Yes, I'm aware of all that, Isla, but this is a top-up. A thank you for all that you've been doing. And before you ask, Ellen is in full agreement.'

She hugged him and didn't argue any more. It felt good to be appreciated and valued and her bank balance was alarmingly low at present.

'Now, we're popping off to Bexhill tomorrow, but we'll be back in good time for the meet and greet,' John said. 'You're welcome to join us.'

'No, I think you ought to go on your own and spend some quality time with her. Obviously, I'll get to see Gran whilst you're away, in between courses. I think I ought to get on with Jerome Rowley's painting tomorrow afternoon.'

'OK.' He turned to go and then stopped in his tracks. 'Oh, I nearly forgot to give you this.' Isla had wondered what was in the large brown envelope he had set down on the dressing table. He handed it to her.

'I rescued it from the skip when Ellen was sorting out your grandmother's house. I could see it was full of photographs and ephemera. I've been keeping it safe in the workshop and had almost forgotten about it. Thought you might like to take a look. Your Gran might appreciate some of it being put into an album.'

'Oh, John, what a good idea! That was thoughtful of you. Perhaps Gran and I can sort through it together.'

The following afternoon, Isla went off to Rowley Grange. She was dreading running into Jed, although he hadn't been in church that morning. She had been working for quite a while when he appeared unexpectedly and stood gazing over her shoulder.

'You've breathed life into that picture,' he told her.

'Mm, another session like this and I'll be able to finish it off at home.'

He was standing so close to her that her heartbeat quickened. He wasn't to know the effect he had on her. She set down her brushes and hoped he didn't notice her hand was shaking.

'Did you want something, Jed?'

There was a glint in his green eyes. 'Why did you let me kiss you, when all the time you were still seeing Dom?' he asked abruptly.

'Because I — because . . . I've told you there's nothing going on between Dom and me.'

'It didn't look like it,' he told her stonily.

The colour stained her cheeks. 'If you must know, we'd just been out to celebrate Amy's engagement to Dale.'

His eyes widened. 'Amy got engaged to Dale. When was this?'

'A couple of weeks back, on her birthday. Anyway, Dom drove me back and . . . '

'Yes, I saw. He'd obviously enjoyed the occasion. He looked pleased with himself for the rest of the afternoon. You seem to have that effect on men, Isla.'

'Well, really! That's rich coming from you. You're pretty free with your kisses too.'

She saw the colour stain his cheeks and wished she could retract the remark. Slowly, she picked up her brushes and began to pack away.

Jerome appeared on the steps and waved. 'Are you coming in for tea, Isla?'

'Not this afternoon, thank you, Jerome. I've got a few things to do before the meet and greet.'

'I'll see you there later,' Jed told her, 'and I'm sorry if I misjudged the situation the other day in the rose garden.'

And, not waiting for her reply, he left her side and crossing the lawn, practically ran up the steps and into the house.

But you didn't, she wanted to call after him. That kiss had made her realise what love really was, and now Dom had managed to spoil things. Tears blurred her vision as she packed away her painting things. It didn't make any difference anyway; not when Nicole was around to distract Jed.

★   ★   ★

To Isla's relief, the final group of students for the pottery group were equally as delightful and cooperative as the first group had been, although they were of an intermediate standard. They were keen to learn and willing to help anyone who was experiencing difficulty. Isla found herself thoroughly enjoying the course and hoped she could keep up the momentum when John departed.

Several of the students were from John and Sam's previous classes, but there were also a few who had attended other college courses and wanted to spend more time perfecting what they had learnt or finish off projects.

'There's some real talent in this group and their work is so individual, John.'

'Yes, it's a pity I won't be here to see it through. Now, Sam will be here tomorrow, but is there anything you need to know before I disappear?'

She grinned, 'Plenty. I think I could learn a lot from this group.'

He patted her shoulder. 'You'll cope. I've got every faith in you.'

⋆　⋆　⋆

On Thursday, Sam was already there when Isla arrived at the Arts Centre, having said her goodbyes to John and Ellen. The students spent the morning decorating opaque white tin-glazed tiles, which some of them had prepared already in John's other classes.

He had left some ready for those

students who needed them. The technique, known as *Majolica*, had been used for centuries in Europe, with roots in the Medieval Islamic World. John showed them how to apply decoration using various brushes, a sponge and open-weave material.

'The sponges add texture as well,' Sam explained.

After lunch, Sam gave them a short lecture about various other forms of simple decoration that they could think about using, illustrated with photographs on the screen. They were then given time to get on with their various projects.

'So far, so good,' Sam said at the end of the day. 'They're a nice bunch, aren't they?'

'They certainly are. I'm impressed with what they're doing.'

'Now, tomorrow, we're going to try our hand at *Sgraffito* — are you familiar with that?'

'I think so. I've seen John's demonstration with the previous group, and

I've attempted it in the past myself. It's a technique used in decoration which involves scratching or incising through a coloured slip or glaze.'

Sam slapped her on the shoulder. 'You've got it! It reveals a different colour underneath. Anyway, there are worksheets and a short film to begin with.'

Jed appeared in the doorway at that moment. 'Sorry, I haven't had a chance to pop in before. How's it gone?'

After filling him in, Sam left the centre and for a moment there was a silence.

Jed cleared his throat. 'Dad's out tonight so I'm going to eat here with the residents. I have it on the best authority from Aunty June, who's doing kitchen duty, that it's chicken casserole. I don't suppose — that is — you'd be welcome to join us.'

'Oh, I, um . . . ' He gave her one of his smiles and her knees felt weak. She realised that he was offering her an olive branch. 'That would be lovely,' she told him, her treacherous heart beating wildly.

'Great. I'll see you around six thirty.'

She rushed home to have a shower and wash her hair, then changed into a denim skirt and embroidered white top.

There was only a small group of residents, because quite a few of the students this week had opted to come in daily. Those that were resident joined together with the other course members who were doing silk-painting that week. Angela Foster, their tutor, was also staying on for the meal.

As Jed had promised, the food was delicious, and Aunty June was in her element as she bustled about, helping the other ladies in the kitchen.

Isla couldn't have wished for a nicer bunch of students. They sat over coffee for a long while until one of the older ladies gave a prodigious yawn and got to her feet.

'Time to call it a night, I think,' she said, and several others also got to their feet to return to their respective guest houses. Angela got up too. Some of the younger students decided to sample the nightlife in one of the nearby towns. They invited Jed and Isla along, but Jed cried off, saying he had to lock up and do a few things back at the Grange. Isla declined too, needing to look over Sam's notes for the following day.

When they were alone, Jed caught her hands between his and leant towards her, his eyes bright and full of meaning. Her heart hammered and it was as if an electric charge shot along her arm at his contact.

'Isla, I just wanted to say . . . '

But before he could finish his sentence, the door flew open to admit Dominic, red in the face from hurrying.

'Oh, thank goodness you're still here, Jed!' He didn't seem to notice Isla.

'What's the matter? Has something happened to my father?' Jed demanded.

'No, nothing like that. It's the computer! I've lost some important information that you need to take to London next week, and I've been trying for ages to retrieve it but . . . '

Jed murmured something rude beneath his breath, and catching Isla's reproach-ful eye, apologised. 'OK, Dom, calm down. I'll come and take a look as soon as I've locked up here. Sorry Isla. Sounds like a crisis. So, what's new?'

As she drove back to Ivy Cottage, Isla wondered what the problem was and hoped it could be resolved. The contact of Jed's hands on hers had taken her breath away. If only Dom hadn't inter-rupted at that precise moment. Now she would have to wait to learn what Jed had been about to say.

* * *

The following morning when Isla arrived at the Arts Centre, there was no sign of Sam or Jed, and the door was locked. Shortly afterwards, Angela appeared laden with materials. She frowned.

'Where is everyone? Did you all go on the razzle last night?'

'No — at least, some of the

youngsters did, but Dominic Irwin had a serious problem with the computer in the office and Jed went off to help him.'

Angela put down her armful of materials and struggled to extract her mobile from her skirt pocket. A moment later, she was speaking to Jed.

'He's on his way,' she said. 'Not like him to be late, and I wonder where Sam's got to?'

Jed appeared before long, looking uncharacteristically dishevelled. His hair was tousled, and he was unshaven.

'Sorry folk. I was up until the small hours with a computer glitch,'

As he unlocked the outer door, Isla couldn't resist a smile.

'What?' he demanded irritably.

'I was just recalling your comments about artist's attire.'

He looked down at his crumpled T-shirt. 'Yes, well, Dom and I didn't get much sleep.'

'Did you fix the problem?'

'Hopefully, with the aid of some whiskey and several cups of black coffee. 'It was a bit of a nightmare. Anyway, I'm off to see if I can make myself look halfway presentable.' He frowned as he caught sight of the clock. 'I wonder where Sam's got to this morning?'

As if in answer to his question, his mobile rang at that moment. He whipped it out of his pocket. Angela mouthed to Isla that she was going to her room and disappeared.

'I don't believe this,' Jed said. 'That was Sam. Mollie's had a fall and, although he doesn't think she's broken anything, he's taken her to A&E to have her checked over — just to be on the safe side. Can you hold the fort for a while just until I make myself present-able and have a spot of breakfast?'

'Of course. Don't rush back on my account. There's a short film and the students will set that up. I know roughly what we are supposed to be doing for the rest of this morning.'

He gave her one of his smiles. 'Thanks Isla. You're a star. If you're sure, I'll leave you to it for the time being. Here come some of your students.'

It was practically breaktime before Jed returned, looking his usual immaculate self once more. He moved from one group of students to the next. They were engrossed in what they were doing, and Isla was inwardly relieved. Finally, he stopped by her side.

'Well, you've obviously got everything under control.' He smelt of some woody fragrance, his hair was newly washed, and he no longer looked as if he'd been up half the night.

'Actually, I think I preferred the bohemian, artistic look,' she told him *sotto voce*, and his mouth twitched.

'Watch what you're saying, young woman, or I'll give you the sack,' he whispered back, and she chuckled.

During the coffee break, Angela's group joined them. Sam texted to say that he was still waiting for Mollie to be x-rayed. After the break, Jed went off with Angela to take a look at what her group were doing.

Isla's students were making good progress with the *Sgraffito*. The more advanced amongst them were also taking it in turns on the two potter's wheels. Towards lunchtime, Jed appeared again, and stood watching as Isla gave a demonstration to those in the group who were still finding the process of throwing clay difficult. Patiently, she showed them once more how to throw a shallow open form which she then turned into a bowl.

She was fully aware that Jed was standing there, but didn't dare look up, afraid that she would lose her concentration.

'Bravo,' he applauded as she completed the task. He did a tour of the room again, looking at what the students had achieved that morning, before ending up beside her.

'You've done well, but I'm afraid we've got an on-going problem because Sam can't see his way clear to coming in at all today. Now, do you have any idea what this lot are supposed to be doing this afternoon?'

Isla swallowed. 'I think Sam was intending to give them a talk on various other techniques for decoration. We made a start yesterday and covered some of them, but he must have taken his notes with him.'

'Oh, that's not helpful.' He frowned. 'If all else fails, I suppose we could take them to the local museum to take a look at ancient pottery.'

She raised her eyebrows. 'Oh, I think we can do better than that. I sat in on one or two of John's talks last time and could waffle my way through with the aid of some illustrations. I've got quite a few notes of my own. Several of the students are keen to complete their own projects, and decoration is the next stage. They've also got their portfolios to work on.'

'Mm, but perhaps they'll need something with a bit more substance.'

Her eyes widened. She was about to tell him he was a hard taskmaster but, seeing the glint in his eyes, thought better of it.

'Yes, well, I thought anyone who wanted to could have a go at producing some stamps from modelled clay coils or try other means, such as pressing or rolling onto textured materials. We've got a lot of items available for them to use.'

He frowned. 'But wouldn't they have done that before, when they were beginners?'

She shrugged. 'Probably, but it doesn't hurt to refresh their memories, and it's doubtful that they would have made the stamps, because they tend to be too fiddly for beginners.'

'OK, so you've convinced me. Anyway, *practise makes perfect*, as they say.'

Relieved that he seemed satisfied, she looked down at the notes in her hand that she'd fortunately made the previous day. 'The other thing Sam has got lined up is for them to draw onto the surfaces of bowls or tiles that have already been biscuit-fired. Some of the students have already done that in his previous classes in preparation for this course. It might be an idea if all of them could do some preliminary sketches.'

'Well, there seem to be plenty of ideas there for them to choose from. How about I come in to assist with your talk?'

She swallowed. 'If you like.'

His eyes glinted dangerously. 'I do like, and so I will.'

The students were very cooperative and happy with the work she had arranged for them. She was halfway through her talk and beginning to think Jed had decided not to put in an appearance after all, when he slipped into the room, sitting unobtrusively at the back as she expounded on some of the more intricate forms of decoration.

In addition to burnishing and banding, she included applied and pierced decoration. She had several illustrations to accompany her talk and ended by showing examples of decorating white-glazed surfaces with a combination of drawing and painting techniques, which is what the students were hoping to do the following day.

The group obviously found the talk interesting and asked some intelligent questions. Jed added to some of her answers with one or two comments of his own.

'I thought you were going to take a part of the talk yourself,' she said, as they stopped for a tea-break before the final session.

'You were coping so well that there was really no need. I'm sorry I doubted you in the very beginning. You are obviously very competent.'

The colour stained her cheeks. 'I aim to please,' she said lightly.

'And you certainly do,' he assured her.

The last session went equally as well. Jed spent a bit of time with Angela and then returned to Isla for the remainder of the afternoon. He gave helpful advice to those in the group who were working on drawings to copy onto their pottery the following morning, and helped anyone experiencing problems when trying their hand at the potter's wheel. He did it in such a way that he instilled confidence into the student and Isla, glancing in his direction from time to time, soon realised that he was a gifted and experienced teacher. He also took some of them over to the kiln room to instruct them on how to load and unload it.

'Well, we got through that without any mega problems, didn't we?' he said to Isla when everyone had gone and they were tidying the room. 'Hopefully, Sam will be back tomorrow. His sister-in-law is coming to stay with Mollie for a couple of days. She definitely hasn't broken anything, but she's very shaken up and rather bruised.'

'Oh, that's such a pity. Sam said she was having a good patch this week,' Isla told him sympathetically.

'Yes, she doesn't have an easy time of it. Now, Dad's covering here tonight. Fancy coming for a walk to shake away the cobwebs? It's been quite a day.'

They walked through the wood again

to the meadow. The flowers were beginning to close up, but they stood and watched as rabbits bobbed to and fro with a flash of their white powder-puff tails.

'I know they're a farmer's nightmare, but you have to admit they're cute,' Isla said. 'I used to love my *Peter Rabbit* book when I was a kid.'

'They're not doing any harm here,' Jed conceded. 'Changing the subject — are you busy on Sunday, Isla?'

'Not particularly, why?'

'I wondered if you'd care to come with me for the visit to Barns Cross. Unless, of course, you had other plans.'

Her heart missed a beat. 'No, that would be great. I need to visit Gran soon but next week will be fine.'

'Right. Only I wouldn't want to prevent you from going out with Dom,' he said, watching her intently for her reaction. He didn't expect the one he received.

'I have absolutely no plans to go out with Dom on Sunday or any other day,' she assured him furiously. 'I don't know what I have to do to convince you that Dom and I are just good friends.'

'You could have fooled me; but then I suppose it depends how you interpret the word *good*,' he told her. 'From where I was sitting the other day, it looked rather more than that.'

'You are despicable, Jed Rowley!' she told him, and rushing at him, pummelled his chest with her fists.

'Hey!' he protested, and catching her wrists, bent his head and kissed her hard on the mouth. He then released her so abruptly that she staggered backwards.

'So how did that rate, I wonder?' he enquired, and marched off across the meadow.

'Jed,' she shouted after him, and then as he didn't turn round, she said to herself, *Jed, that really was unbelievably good!*

'Jed!' she shouted after him again, but still he ignored her and continued walking at a brisk pace until he practically disappeared from view and was just a dot on the horizon. She dropped down on her knees amongst the wildflowers, the tears streaming down her face. How come he was so bothered about that kiss Dom had given her, when he was obviously still involved with Nicole?

She didn't know how long she remained there, but suddenly a hand touched her gently on the shoulder. Looking up, she saw that Jed had returned.

'I'm sorry, Isla, that was unforgivable of me.' He helped her to her feet, and she leant against his shoulder. He removed the buckle from her hair, letting it flow around her shoulders and buried his head in it.

'I'm sorry too,' she sniffed. 'You shouldn't jump to conclusions.'

They walked down to the brook hand in hand, but this time took the path in the opposite direction, away from the bridge leading to the chalet. There were reeds at the far side of the water, which was crystal clear that evening, and alive with the sound of waterfowl.

'Am I forgiven?' he wanted to know.

'For the time being.' She wanted to mention Nicole, but the words stuck in her throat.

'I like a woman with spirit, but I have to say you have hidden depths, Isla. You pack a good punch as well as being feisty.'

'I did a few self-defence classes a while back,' she admitted sheepishly. 'I promise I won't do that again.'

'Phew, that's a relief, or I might have to wear a protective vest. So, to go back to my original question before I was so rudely interrupted: do you want to come to Barns Cross on Sunday, to see if you can track down your ancestors — and mine of course? I promise to be on my best behaviour.'

She smiled up at him. 'Yes, I'd love to come, but you know what? I think I preferred it when you were behaving just a little bit badly. And in answer to your question, your kiss was *unbelievably good.*'

For answer, he took her in his arms and kissed her again, gently this time, and she knew without a shadow of doubt then that she had fallen hopelessly in love with him.

13

Sam was back the following day and commended Isla for holding the fort so well during his absence. Apparently, Jed had filled him in with what had taken place. The rest of the course went smoothly, and Isla was sorry when it ended. Of the three, she had enjoyed that one the most.

'Jed's taking me to Barns Cross tomorrow,' she told Sam as they put the finishing touches to the exhibition.

He stopped what he was doing. 'Jed is? Well, that's a turn-up for the books.'

Isla stared at him in surprise. 'Why do you say that?'

'Well, he doesn't have the happiest of memories of the place and has frequently said his home is in Woodbridge now.'

'People change,' Isla said, pausing to look at a display. 'It's only now that I've wanted to see where I spent the first couple of years of my life.'

'Does Ellen know you're going?' Sam enquired.

'No, this is something I need to do for myself. There are things I need to know about my past, and Barns Cross seems a good place to start.'

Sam was giving her a strange look. 'Then I hope you will find what you're looking for.'

* * *

The fish and chip supper that evening was an enjoyable occasion. It was just a pity that neither John nor Sam was there. Afterwards, the students took to the floor again and Jed and Isla danced together several times. She knew there was chemistry between them and was determined to make the most of any time they spent together.

'You two seem to be getting on well,' Angela commented, when Jed took a turn round the floor with one of the more mature students.

'We're just colleagues,' Isla said, not wanting any gossip, but feeling a little guilty as she uttered the words.

Angela studied her nails, which were blue and silver. 'I suppose you've met Nicole?'

'Several times — why?'

'Oh, I just wondered. Jed is a very good-looking man, and I wouldn't want you to get hurt. That's all.'

'Thanks for the warning, Angela, but I'm quite capable of taking care of myself,' Isla said, inwardly seething. There was something about the other woman that she didn't care for. From the little time Isla had spent with her, she had found her to be bossy and competitive. Isla knew that she was divorced. Surely she didn't have designs on Jed herself?

* * *

When Isla got home that evening, she remembered the envelope John had given her just before he'd left for New

Zealand. She hadn't had the opportunity to look at the contents, but perhaps she might find something connected with Barns Cross and where she had lived as a small child. It might make sense if she looked before the following day. She should have checked her birth certificate, which she seemed to remember bore the Barns Cross address too, but John had put it in the safe and she didn't know the combination.

She made herself a mug of hot chocolate and curled up on the sofa, tipping out the contents of the envelope. She didn't know a lot of the people in the photographs, but there were a few of her grandparents, plus Ellen and her mother, presumably when they were teenagers. At the bottom of the pile, she discovered several postcards and, turning them over, discovered they had been sent to an address in Barns Cross: Number 3, Lynden Villas.

The following morning, after church, Jed and Isla set off for Barns Cross.

'I don't suppose you've got any clue

as to where your family lived?'

'Actually, yes, I have.' Isla told him about the envelope John had rescued from the skip and produced the postcard with the address on it from her bag. 'It was 3, Lynden Villas,' she told him.

'Hmm, that doesn't ring any bells; we'll have to ask around. You've said it's on the east side of the village, so that narrows it down.'

Barns Cross, when they reached it, was disappointing. Isla hadn't known what to expect, but this was no more than a long, straggling street. There was a general store and post-office, a pub and a church. Near the church was a small green with the cross which Isla assumed had given the village its name; although now it looked as if it was a war memorial.

As they passed the church, a sign proclaimed that it was open that afternoon.

'That's fortuitous; perhaps there will be someone there who remembers your family.'

Jed pulled into the car park of the Golden Lion public house and Isla looked at him enquiringly.

'I thought we'd eat first and then begin our search. I have it on the best authority that this pub is renowned for its Sunday lunches and it's my shout.'

The lunch lived up to expectation: roast beef, Yorkshire pudding and all the trimmings. Isla and Jed talked about art exhibitions they had visited and discovered a lot about each other's likes and dislikes. It seemed that Jed quite liked cooking when he had time. Isla told him how much she enjoyed gardening, and that she was going to love having a free hand whilst Ellen and John were away.

'Dessert?' he enquired as the waiter removed their plates.

'Oh, I really don't think I could manage another mouthful.'

'How about a raspberry sorbet and coffee?' he enquired. 'That's what I'm going to have.'

She grinned. 'Go on then, you've

twisted my arm.'

As they were leaving the pub, they encountered Angela Foster, accompanied by a middle-aged man, crossing the carpark.

'Well, fancy seeing you!' Angela exclaimed.

'Yes, what an amazing coincidence,' Jed said lightly. 'Enjoy your lunch.'

'Oh, I'm sure we will.' Angela didn't introduce them to her companion. Isla could tell that Jed was put out that they'd run into them and wondered why.

Presently, they crossed to the little church. The vicar was there but said he hadn't been in the area long enough to help them, although perhaps another time, if they phoned him in advance, they could take a look at the church records. Isla was looking round her, aware that her grandmother would have been a member of the congregation many years ago, when a middle-aged woman with short, bleached hair approached her.

'I couldn't help overhearing. You said you were looking into your family history and mentioned Martha and Harry Milne.'

'Yes, they're my grandparents. They lived at the east end of Barns Cross.'

'Yes, I know — in Lynden Villas. I'm Sonia Sadler. I was at school with their daughter, Ellen.'

Isla's eyes widened. 'Really! She's my aunt.'

'Then you must be Leona's little girl, all grown up now.'

'Yes, I'm Isla Milne.' She saw the woman's expression.

'I was sorry to learn what happened, my dear — a tragic accident.'

Isla swallowed. 'Yes, it was.'

'Such a pretty girl, your mother. You look very much like her, my dear. So, she didn't marry, then?'

'No,' Isla said shortly. 'My grandmother's in a residential home in Bexhill now and my grandfather died several years ago. I thought it would be interesting to take a look around the village and see the house where I spent the first two years of my life. Perhaps you could point me in the general direction of my grandparents' old home.'

The woman nodded and told Isla how to find Lynden Villas. 'Actually, I think you might find some Milnes are buried in the churchyard. Oh, and one of your ancestors is named on the War Memorial on the village green.'

'Really? I'd no idea.' She thanked the woman and, shortly afterwards, Jed joined her from the opposite side of the church, where he'd been examining some brass rubbings.

They went outside and discovered two graves belonging to the Milne family: Isla's great-grandparents, and some great-aunts and uncles. She knew that her grandmother had only moved into the village when she got married, so there wouldn't be any from her side of the family.

'Well, that's made coming here worthwhile,' Isla commented. A few minutes later Jed stopped in front of another grave. The inscription on the stone bore the names: *Hilda and Frank Platt.*

'My grandparents on my mother's side,' he told her.

'Actually, Hilda Platt was a friend of my Gran's,' Isla said. 'She happened to mention it the other week.'

'Really? It's a small world. So, did your grandmother also mention that Hilda's daughter, Irene, my mother, now resides in Scotland with my father's cousin, Edward?' he asked sharply.

'Not exactly. She knew Irene Platt had married a Rowley but wasn't sure if it was Jerome. It was actually Amy Bradshaw's grandmother who supplied that piece of information.'

Jed sighed. 'It was inevitable someone would say something, I suppose. The Rowleys' past is fairly colourful. Let's take a look at the war memorial, shall we?'

They went across to the village green and stood in silence for a moment or two, studying the names. Isla picked out a Walter Milne who had died in the First World War, and Jed then pointed to one of his own ancestors, a Daniel Rowley.

Leaving the green, they walked round the side of the church to see the village school which Ellen and Leona Milne, and John Ainsworth had attended.

'My mother came here, too,' Jed told her. 'Actually, I did as well, for a short while — until I got sent to prep school.'

'Really? It looks a lovely little school. I wonder if my grandfather came here. We've obviously got more in common than we realise.'

Presently, they wandered back to the carpark then drove the short distance to the east side of Barns Cross. They pulled up in front of Lynden Villas, where a middle-aged lady was busy doing some gardening next door to number three.

She looked up as the car approached. Getting out, Isla explained who she was.

'Oh, I'm afraid you've just missed Mum's neighbours. I am sure they would have been most interested to have met you. You might have been disappointed though because these places aren't a bit like they used to be. They've been renovated recently — and about time too! Actually, this is my mother's house, but I grew up here and remember your family. Mum would love to talk with you. She's sitting out the back. Come round. I'm Joy, by the way.'

Ruby Crane was sitting on the patio crocheting blanket squares. She was a little younger than Martha Milne. Joy introduced them.

'Oh, my goodness, I remember your grandparents and Ellen and Leona. You can't be Leona's daughter!'

'I am.' Isla told her smilingly.

'Well, fancy that! Come and sit down, the pair of you. Joy will make us some tea and we can have a chat. Joy, you remember Ellen and Leona, don't you?'

'Yes, of course, although Ellen was older and Leona slightly younger.' An uncertain expression flitted across Joy's face.

'She died,' Isla said, realising that, like Sonia Sadler, this was what Joy was trying to remember.

Ruby set down her crocheting. 'We used to keep in touch regularly, but you know how it is. Martha only came to visit a few times after moving to Bexhill and she always came on her own.' Her attention suddenly turned to Jed. 'I feel I ought to know you, too.'

'That's because I used to live on the west side of Barns Cross. I'm Jerome Rowley's son.'

Light dawned. 'You're Jerome Junior, of course.'

'Jed, please,' he corrected her, and Isla hid a smile. She had wondered if *Jed* was short for *Jerome*: a family name that he obviously tried not to admit to.

They spent a lovely hour with Ruby Crane, who told Isla a lot about her mother. Isla hoped she would remember it all when she got back to Woodbridge.

'You were such a gorgeous baby,' Ruby said. 'Of course, Leona was very attractive, and you're so much like her.'

'So I've been told before.' Isla sipped her tea thoughtfully.

'Of course, Leona was very young when you were born.'

Isla nodded. 'Nearly nineteen. She wasn't much older than me when she died.'

'Did your father . . . ?'

'No,' Isla said. 'He probably isn't even aware of my existence.'

'Oh, my dear; we always wondered . . . '

'Mum,' Joy said, giving her a warning look, and then making a great show of passing round the biscuits.

Isla wished she could pluck up the courage to ask what they had *always wondered*. Had they got any inkling of who her father had been?

'These things happen,' she said, filling an awkward silence. 'I was virtually brought up by my grandparents because my mother was working — so I didn't miss out. I had a happy childhood until I was twelve.'

Shortly afterwards, Jed and Isla got to

their feet. Shaking hands all round, they were invited to call again if they were in the area. They spent a few moments looking over the fence into the immaculate garden of number three and made their way back to the car.

'Well, that was interesting,' Jed remarked.

'It certainly was,' Isla agreed, not sure how she felt about the visit, which had thrown up unanswered questions again.

'So, you don't know who your father is?' Jed pressed gently.

'No, and I'm not sure I want to anymore,' Isla told him.

'Well, if it's any consolation, I know who my mother is, and she doesn't seem to want anything to do with me either.'

'But you've got a father who obviously cares about you.'

He nodded. 'True. We have our differences from time to time, but usually manage to compromise. Now, are you ready to go back to Woodbridge or is there anything else you'd like to see whilst you're here?'

'Actually, there is one other thing — if you wouldn't mind very much.'

'Of course not. I'm not in any particular hurry. What is it?'

She hesitated, and then said in a rush, 'I was wondering — could we take a look at the house where you used to live?'

He looked startled. 'Well, yes, I suppose so. Why would you want to do that?'

'Just so that I could understand a bit more about you I suppose.'

'Well, in that case, we'll go and take a look.'

'Of course, I have learnt something else about you this afternoon . . . 'she said, grinning.

'Go on,' he challenged, his green eyes glinting dangerously.

'You're not Jed at all — you're Jerome.'

He grimaced. 'As a matter of fact — if you really want to know, Jed is an abbreviation of my full name which is Jerome Edward Daniel!'

'There's really nothing I can say to that,' she said, laughing. 'Jed is a great deal more suitable for an artist, after all. Saves you getting mixed up with the literary world.'

He chuckled, 'Actually, I enjoyed reading *Three Men in a Boat*, although I don't believe I'm Jerome K. Jerome's namesake. Anyway, what about you? I've been wondering if you're a descendant of A.A. Milne — creator of *Winnie the Pooh*.'

'Much as I'd like to claim that I am, sadly, I can't find any connection.'

They laughed and he started up the car. They drove back through the village again and up the slight incline on the west side. Presently, he pulled up beside a large house behind a neat yew hedge.

'It's lovely,' she said. 'So, who lives there now?'

'Would you believe me if I said I'm not too sure? It was left to Dad's cousin, Edward, when my grandfather died, but when he went off to Scotland with my mother, his wife carried on living there for a while longer. Maybe one of the cousins is still in residence.'

'Don't you know?' she asked incredulously.

He shook his head. 'It wouldn't be difficult to find out, but I'm not particularly interested. Sometimes it's best to make a clean break. It causes less heartache that way.'

They sat looking at the house for a few minutes longer before he drove them home. It had been a strange sort of day, she reflected, but she was glad she had made the journey to Barns Cross. She was none the wiser about her father, but it didn't seem to matter so much.

She declined Jed's offer to have tea at Rowley Grange, and he bent over and kissed her lightly on the cheek before dropping her off at Ivy Cottage.

⋆ ⋆ ⋆

'So, what else did you do in Barns Cross?' Martha Milne's bright blue eyes

295

looked at her granddaughter expectantly. Isla was frankly surprised. Martha had been decidedly grouchy when she'd arrived, as she'd been suffering from a slight cold for a couple of days. Instead of chiding her about the visit at the weekend as Isla expected, the old lady had bucked up when she'd mentioned it and seemed keen to hear every last detail.

'Actually, we went to take a look at 3 Lynden Villas. The present occupants were out, so we had a nice chat with Ruby Crane and her daughter, Joy.'

'Ruby still lives there! Fancy that. We lost touch over the years. I'd love to see her again, but don't suppose I ever shall. Perhaps I'll give her a ring sometime. Wasn't Jed Rowley bored with all your reminiscing?'

'No — he joined in. After all, he lived in Barns Cross for a good few years himself. Afterwards, we went to look at the place where he used to live.'

'Did he mention his mother and what happened?'

'Only briefly. He doesn't have anything to do with her, which I find sad.'

Martha Milne looked at her, head on one side. 'Mm. He sounds a nice young man. I don't suppose he'd come and visit me one day? I'd like to meet him.'

Isla stared at her grandmother. 'Oh, I — I'm not sure, Gran. He's my employer's son, remember.'

'And I knew him when he wore short trousers,' she retorted.

Isla had to laugh. 'I'll see what I can do. I'm not making any promises, mind.'

She didn't want Jed to think she'd read too much into their relationship or had got the wrong impression. She might have fallen in love with him, and was enjoying spending time with him, but she wasn't under any illusions. She was going to have to pull herself together and accept the fact that he already had a lady friend — the elegant Nicole Trent. It was no good living in cloud cuckoo land, and she had to face up to reality and do the right thing however hard it might prove to be.

By the time she'd gone through some of the contents of the envelope of memorabilia that John had salvaged from the skip, Gran had cheered up considerably. She wanted to keep most of it, and Isla had the idea that she could get an album and they could assemble it together.

'And don't forget what I said about bringing Jed Rowley with you another time,' her grandmother told her as they parted company. As if she needed reminding, Isla thought grimly. How was she going to get out of that one?

*   *   *

Isla managed to fit in another afternoon's painting at the Grange on Wednesday. Hopefully, she had done enough to work on it at home. She was pleased with what she had achieved so far. She was just about to pack away when Jed came up the drive, this time on foot. She hadn't seen him since Sunday.

'Are you coming or going?' he wanted to know.

'Going actually. I've been here most of the afternoon.'

He peered over her shoulder. 'That is beautiful. Dad is going to love it.'

'Good! I didn't have a very good beginning, but things have got progressively better.'

'Nicole smudged your first attempt, didn't she?' he said, giving her a knowing glance.

'How did . . . ? I'm sure it was an accident,' she blustered.

'I'm not,' he said grimly. 'There was rather a lot of blue paint on her fingers and, anyway, I saw her leaning over your painting, so don't make excuses for her.'

'I don't think she believes our relationship is purely professional,' Isla told him.

'Well, she'd be right there, wouldn't she?' His green eyes danced with amusement.

Before Isla could think of a suitable

reply, Dominic appeared on the steps and beckoned to Jed urgently. Once he had gone, she finished packing away her things, gathered up her easel and went off to her car.

Her heart was heavy as she drove back to Ivy Cottage. Did Jed just view her as someone to amuse him when he had some free time? She knew she was being a fool to encourage him, and should know better, but she couldn't seem to help herself. She had never felt so deeply about anyone before.

That evening, Jed phoned her. 'Isla, I'm sorry we were interrupted. I had to attend to something urgently in the office and, by the time I'd finished, you'd packed up and gone.'

'That's OK,' she assured him. 'Did you want something?'

'I haven't been to The Hawthorns for a while — the residential home in Rowley Manor. I had a phone call from the manager, asking if there was any possibility of fitting in a craft session for the residents.'

'Oh, I remember you telling me about it,' she said, immediately interested.

'Would you care to come along? You've only recently had all the necessary checks, haven't you?'

'I certainly have, and I certainly would. When is this?'

'It's short notice I'm afraid — Friday morning. They had a craft morning planned but the person taking it is ill. We'll be decorating pottery mugs. It'll be a very small group — eight at the most — and one or two of the carers will be there, too.'

Jed sounded at his most professional, and she knew she'd love just being with him.

Friday was a fun morning. The elderly residents were positively delightful, and it was so rewarding. They were very enthusiastic, and one or two mugs got broken because of shaky hands, but none of this mattered. They all had a sense of achievement.

'We've had a lovely time, dear,' one

old gentleman told her. 'You remind me of my granddaughter. She's at university and I don't get to see her too often. When this mug is ready, I'm going to give it to her.'

'Come again soon,' an elderly lady said, planting a kiss on Jed's cheek.

'I will,' he promised, and after a quick coffee in the manager's office, he and Isla left the building.

'I enjoyed that,' she told him, and taking a deep breath, she mentioned what her grandmother had said on Tuesday about wanting to meet Jed.

'Of course, I'll come with you. I'd love to meet your grandmother. She sounds an absolute character and actually, I feel I know her already, after all you've told me about her,' he assured her. 'Anyway, the more I think about it, the more I think I might have met her in Barns Cross years ago when I was a teenager — probably at some function. After all, she was friendly with *my* grandmother.'

'So she was. Perhaps at some point

we could arrange to do a pottery decoration class at Gran's home, too.'

'Well, if you think it would be welcome then I'm all for it. You saw how everyone enjoyed themselves this morning.'

It had been a lovely morning. Isla loved working with Jed and wished that the summer could go on for ever.

14

The first of Isla's two painting courses got off the ground the following week. She was in her element. This was something she felt confident with. She had lots of ideas and spent the first session finding out what the students wanted from the course and giving them an illustrated talk about the various media they might use. She had enjoyed the pottery courses, but she loved drawing and painting most of all. The thought that she could ignite a spark within someone and inspire them to create a picture thrilled her.

She had been surprised to discover that Jed was running the parallel course that week, and the thought of spending so much time with him excited her. She knew that she should control her emotions, but it was difficult. Any time she spent with him was precious, and she would treasure the memories.

During the break she went to talk to a couple who had enrolled late, bringing the number on her course up to twelve.

She looked at the paperwork in her hand. James and Julie Westfield. It seemed to be a popular surname. Something suddenly dawned on her.

'Are you by any chance related to Sam Westfield?' she asked James.

He smiled. 'Actually, I'm Sam's brother. I've always wanted to have another go at painting and drawing so when he told me you were running this course and there were still some spaces, I persuaded Julie to come along. Your reputation's gone before you.'

'Well, let's hope the course lives up to your expectations. You'll be given the opportunity of experimenting with a number of different mediums this week. After that you can either carry on by yourself or choose to enrol in an evening class.'

'That sounds good — doesn't it, Julie?'

Isla noticed that Julie was far more

reticent, and she merely nodded. Perhaps James' wife had come along against her will.

'Of course, Sam has a tough time of it because his wife, Mollie, has so much ill health. Julie helps out when she can, don't you love?'

Julie looked embarrassed and nodded. Isla went off to speak with some of the other students. She had set up three lots of still life and, after the break, the students split into groups and began to draw using charcoal and oil pastels.

The day passed swiftly, and everyone seemed keen and eager to tackle the task. The end results were mixed. Some students showed a decided talent whilst others had very little skill and their pictures were amateurish.

James Westfield hovered at the end of the afternoon, obviously wanting to ask Isla something, whilst Julie looked distinctly uncomfortable.

'Isla, Sam says your Aunt Ellen used to be married to our cousin Tom.'

'That's right, but it was only for a

short while — around ten years. I remember Tom very well. Sam says he's in Canada nowadays.'

'Yes, with his second wife and their two children.'

Isla swallowed hard. She hadn't been prepared for this. 'Oh, I hadn't realised he had any children. I'm afraid we lost touch, so much so that I mistakenly thought he'd died.'

Julie shot her husband a look. 'Yes, well, your family made it difficult for him to keep in touch or no doubt he would have done. He was devastated when Leona died.'

'We all were,' Isla said, desperately wanting the conversation to end. 'Now, if you'll excuse me, I need to catch Jed Rowley before he leaves. His father is going to be our model for the portrait drawings tomorrow.'

Isla was relieved to get out of the room. There had been something in Julie Westfield's expression that had bothered her. She didn't remember much about her mother's funeral, but she knew Uncle Tom had been there to comfort her. She pulled herself back to the present with difficulty and went in search of Jed.

Isla had been highly amused when she discovered that Jerome Rowley had volunteered to act as a model for her portrait classes the following day. She found him talking with Jed.

'I've come to see that you're still up for being our model tomorrow,' she told him.

'Yes, but there's one stipulation,' Jerome told her firmly.

'OK, what's that?'

Jerome wagged a finger at her. 'That I remain fully clothed, and that means no shorts either.'

Isla tried to keep a straight face but failed when Jed burst out laughing.

'Jerome, I wouldn't dream of asking you to remove any of your clothing apart from perhaps your blazer and tie.'

'And you might need to prise those off him.' Jed said, and laughed again, setting her off.

'When you two have quite finished. A man has his dignity you know,' Jerome said, but there was a twinkle in his eye.

'Well, rest assured that it's only a head and shoulders portrait this week.'

Jerome gave an exaggerated sigh. 'What a pity! I'm wearing my snazzy socks!'

'Did you know that James Westfield is Sam's brother?' Isla asked Jed now.

'Yes. He was so keen to come that Dom enrolled him and his wife at the last minute. I haven't had a chance to tell you. Why? There isn't a problem, is there?'

'I'm not sure, Jed. He made a point of collaring me just now to establish that it was his cousin who had been married to Aunt Ellen. His wife made it sound as if my family prevented Uncle Tom from keeping in touch with any of us.'

'Yes, well they probably thought it was best to have a clean break,' Jerome said, pragmatic as ever.

'Not to the extent of making me

believe that Tom had died, surely? Apparently, he's remarried and has a couple of children.'

'Then I expect Sam and this James have the address, and there's no reason why you shouldn't get in touch if you want to, is there?' Jed pointed out.

'I suppose not. I'll have to think about it.' Deep in thought, Isla went back to her own room.

The following morning, Isla split the students into two groups. One carried on working on the still life but using a different medium, whilst the others began drawings of Jerome. After the break, they swapped over. Jerome thoroughly enjoyed himself but fidgeted rather a lot, so that Isla was obliged to ask him to *please sit still.* He thought the resulting portraits were hilarious — which some of them actually were.

When the day drew to a close, Jerome invited students from both groups to come up to Rowley Grange for a strawberry tea on the terrace the following afternoon.

310

'You're invited too,' Jed told her. 'Dom will be there.'

Isla scowled at him. 'How many more times do I have to tell you that there is absolutely nothing going on between Dom and me?'

He shrugged, and, infuriated, she challenged him. 'Anyway, what about you and Nicole?'

'It was a little complicated, but hopefully that problem's been resolved . . . ' He broke off as a couple of students approached him with a burning issue concerning their jewellery.

'Excuse me, Isla; we'll resume this conversation at a later date.'

He left her wondering what on earth he had been about to say.

Her students spent the following day sketching at different locations around the church. They produced some interesting work. As they were only going to have a cold supper that evening, most of them had accepted Jerome's invitation to tea. The day students had been invited too, and to her surprise, James and Julie

Westfield came along.

Over bowls of strawberries and cream and scones, the groups merged together and chatted. It was a lovely, relaxed occasion, but Isla wondered why Julie Westfield kept exchanging looks with James and then darting glances at her.

When people were beginning to leave, the Westfields came across to her and sat at her table.

James cleared his throat. 'Isla, I hope you don't mind, but there's something we wanted to ask you.'

'About the course?' she questioned, intrigued.

'No, we're both finding that very rewarding. You're such an inspiring tutor. No — it's . . . Oh, dear this is very awkward.'

Julie produced some photographs from her handbag. 'Take a look at these, Isla.'

Puzzled, Isla scanned the photographs and her eyes widened. 'They're pictures of my Uncle Tom and Aunt Ellen and my mother, when they were young. I'm sorry — you've lost me.'

'Now take a look at this photograph of Tom, which he sent to us recently.'

Her brown eyes sparkled. 'Oh, that's a lovely picture and, even though he's aged, I'd have recognised him anywhere.'

'Isla, forgive me for asking this, but you didn't actually know your father, did you?'

Isla was startled; it was hardly the topic of conversation she had expected.

'I'm sorry but I don't see why it is necessary to . . . '

'Forgive me for seeming intrusive. It's Julie who noticed it. Sam tells me you've got your mother's looks and hair colouring, but Julie spotted that your eyes are brown like Sam's, mine and Tom's.'

'And you've got the Westfield nose, too,' Julie added.

'So, what exactly are you saying?' Isla demanded, her heart beating rapidly and a peculiar feeling in her stomach.

'Tom never stopped talking about Leona and how beautiful she was. He'd had a whirlwind romance with Ellen at Art College, but soon after they were married, he discovered it had been a mistake. We've always thought he married the wrong sister.'

It suddenly dawned on Isla what Julie was trying to convey; everything before her seemed to spin and she gripped the sides of the chair. 'No! No! You're the ones that have made a mistake. My mother was already pregnant with me when Ellen got married. I was born a few months later.'

'Exactly,' Julie said, with an air of satisfaction.

It took every ounce of self-control for Isla to get to her feet and say coolly, 'Well, it's an interesting theory, but you have absolutely no proof.'

James caught her hand. 'Isla, if we've got it wrong then I'm sorry, but Julie's right — there *is* a family resemblance. You may not be aware of this, but after Ellen and Tom divorced, Tom went out with Leona. If she hadn't died, then perhaps . . . '

'I think, for the time being at least, the subject is closed,' Isla told them with as much dignity as she could muster. 'Thank you for bringing it to my attention.'

'If you'd rather we didn't finish the course, we'd understand,' Julie told her.

'Absolutely not! I'm sufficiently pro-fessional to be able to keep my personal life separate. Please turn up tomorrow as usual. I just need time to get my head round what you've told me, that's all. I ought to thank you for bringing it out into the open.'

Shortly afterwards, they left, and Jed, who had witnessed the scene, came across. Seeing how distressed Isla was now looking, he took her arm and led her away from anyone in earshot.

'Fancy a walk?' he asked, in such a caring tone that all she could do was nod and fumble for a handkerchief.

They had reached the meadow, and when he asked if she wanted to go on, she nodded. They walked along by the brook to the bridge and crossed to the chalet. It wasn't until they were sitting down at the bench that she was able to tell him what had transpired.

His eyes were full of sympathy. 'I know it's come as a shock, but would it be so very bad if it did turn out that Tom Westfield was your father?'

Isla swallowed. 'I suppose not. I adored Uncle Tom and was so sad when he went away. First, I lost my mother and then, him. But why has everyone kept the truth from me over all these years and why hasn't he kept in touch?'

'Things have changed,' he said gently. 'We live in a different society from the way they were back then. If what James and Julie suspect is true, then it's no wonder your mother didn't want her sister to know that her husband-to-be was your father. She did the honourable thing.'

Isla considered this. 'Do you think I've got a look about me of the Westfields?' she asked.

'Well, you don't have their muscles and your feet are smaller, but . . . '

She was forced to smile. 'Be serious, Jed.'

He surveyed her for a moment. 'OK, now I come to think about it, I suppose that yes, perhaps they do have a point. But, of course, that's only my opinion. Could you ask your grandmother?'

Isla shook her head. 'I wouldn't want to upset her. I've been trying to establish the truth for years, and she hasn't budged an inch. It would answer quite a few questions and, of course, Tom genuinely might not know. I don't want to disrupt his life. You hear all these stories about long-forgotten off-spring suddenly turning up on their parent's doorstep.'

'But no-one seems bothered about the effect all this has had on your life, do they?' he said gently. 'Do you happen to know if your mother had any other boyfriends?'

'She always told me that my father was the love of her life, but that she couldn't tell him about me because of family reasons.'

'Well, there you have it. Of course, if Sam were to e-mail his cousin — get him to phone him . . . '

She shook her head. 'I'm not sure. It's all such a shock. I don't know how I'm going to face James and Julie tomorrow, after that revelation.'

'Shall I ask them not to come?'

She shook her head again. 'No, James has already offered to stay away, but I've told him not to. I can rise above it. We're halfway through the course and personal matters shouldn't be allowed to get in the way of work.'

Coming to sit beside her, he took her in his arms and stroked her hair. 'Well said. If you encounter any problems, just let me know.'

'Mm, I will. And now you can tell me what you started to say about Nicole yesterday.'

'Oh, hopefully it's sorted once and for all. I met Nicole at a party Angela Foster was giving a few months ago. Nicole had just got divorced and I'd split up with my partner. Angela was obviously playing at matchmaking. Nicole latched on to me and kept inviting me to various functions. She's very good at getting her own way and manipulating situations to her own advantage. She accepted invitations on my behalf and turned up at places where she knew I'd be, uninvited. It wasn't always appropriate and could be embarrassing, as you can imagine.'

'I made it clear that, whilst I was happy to be friends and to act as her plus one periodically, that's all it was ever likely to be, but she wouldn't take no for an answer and Angela encouraged her. Nicole had a habit of popping up at the most inopportune moments like the proverbial bad penny. Anyway, I think she's finally got the message.'

'Good, because I think Angela believes you're two-timing Nicole with me.'

'What?' He gave a little incredulous laugh. 'That couldn't be further from the truth. Ever since I met you, Isla, there's only been one woman in my life, but there were a few things I couldn't get out of with Nicole because they were either work-related or had been arranged a while back — like the opera. Believe you me, there was never any deep relationship between us; even though she was extremely flirtatious and couldn't have made it clearer that she wanted there to be. Anyway, I thought you were going out with Dom and was wildly jealous.'

'I'm not a bit like Nicole,' she pointed out.

'No, you're not.' He kissed her then and she gave a little sigh and leant against his shoulder.

'This place has an aura,' she said. 'Do you suppose Tom brought my mother here?'

'Probably. It sounds as if it was love at first sight, but he was already engaged to Ellen.'

She nodded. 'He was my mother's first love. She was barely eighteen. I suppose when Ellen and Tom divorced, they could have had a second chance, but it wasn't to be. Some friends invited her to go on that helicopter ride and . . . '

Isla shuddered and he held her close. 'I'm here for you now, Isla, and we must both move on and put the past behind us.'

★ ★ ★

Isla realised that problems have a habit of resolving themselves. The course drew to a close and the exhibition of work was more than Isla could have hoped for. She parted on good terms with the Westfields and promised to let them know if she learnt anything more about Tom.

The following evening, just as she was thinking of getting an early night, the phone rang. It was John.

'Isla, I'm so glad to have caught you. I haven't got long — Ellen's in the shower.'

'John, what's wrong? Is there a problem?'

'Not exactly, but I've had an e-mail

from Sam. He tells me his brother might have put his foot in it regarding his cousin Tom.'

'Yes, I'm still making my mind up about that — I don't know what to think. Unless . . . John, are you hinting that you might know more than you've led me to believe?'

There was a pause at the end of the line. 'You've remarked that Gran and Ellen seemed to have had a bit of falling-out in recent years?'

'Yes. Things do seem to have been rather strained between them.'

'It was when she was helping your grandmother sort out some papers in the house after your grandfather died. Ellen came across a letter from your mother in the safe. It had been left with her will, but your grandmother had chosen not to say a word about it. She tried taking it back, but Ellen had already read it. The easiest thing would be for you to read it for yourself. It's in our safe at Ivy Cottage with your birth certificate.'

He gave her the combination to the safe and, shortly afterwards, she was aware that Ellen had come into the room. John handed the phone to her, telling her he was ringing up to check on his post. Ellen had a quick word with Isla, saying that she was having an enjoyable time, and checking that all was well with Martha.

With some trepidation, Isla went into the study and managed to open the safe. She found the envelope that John had described to her, and with trembling fingers extracted the letter. It was odd reading the words her mother had penned all those years ago. It told the story she now knew. She got to the last paragraph.

'So, you see, there was no way I could let Ellen down, my darling daughter. I don't regret the affair I had with Tom that summer. I loved him with all my heart, but I loved my sister too. It was best that neither of them knew that I was carrying his *baby on their wedding day.*

'*Don't blame him. I've never told him the truth, although I suppose he must suspect. He's been wonderful to you. I hope that in the future he will take you to our special place — the chalet in the grounds of Rowley Manor, and you'll see where you were conceived through an act of love.*'

The tears streamed down her face. Tom had loved two women. Presently, she pulled herself together and replaced the letter in the safe. She resolved never to let Gran know that she had read it. Her grandmother had wanted to protect both her daughters, after all.

She studied herself in the mirror and realised that the likeness was there for all to see. Ellen must have realised but had chosen not to admit it because the truth was painful. Did that mean that Uncle Tom knew, too?

★   ★   ★

Isla was glad that she had a week before her second painting and drawing course began. Her emotions were in turmoil. So much had happened. She decided to do some more to her painting of Rowley Grange whilst she had the opportunity. Once it was finished, Jed took it off to be framed by a friend of his.

'I'd love to do a painting of the outside of the chalet,' she told Jed and, as he had some time off, he went up there with her, taking his laptop.

It was the most peaceful spot she could have wished for, she decided, as she became totally absorbed in her watercolour. Presently, Jed came outside to see how she was getting on.

'You've captured it so well.'

'I love it here,' she told him simply. 'It's my special place.'

'Our special place,' he corrected gently. He caught her in his arms and kissed her as if he never meant to stop. 'Isla, I've fallen in love with you, my darling girl, and this could be our special place for ever, if you married me.'

She stared at him for a moment and then threw her arms around his neck.

'Oh, Jed, of course I will.'

★ ★ ★

Jerome Rowley could not have been more delighted with their news and insisted on Jed giving Isla an engagement ring that had once belonged to his great grandmother. It was a cluster of diamonds with a large sapphire in the middle and fitted her as if it had been especially made for her.

'But I intend to design and make your wedding ring,' Jed told her.

They went to see Martha Milne the very next day. She was sitting in the garden and her face lit up when they arrived. She was thrilled by Isla's news.

'Oh, this is the very best news I could have!' She looked pensive for a while and presently said, 'Since I've been here, I've had a lot of time on my hands and plenty of time to think. There's something I need to tell you, Isla.'

Jed made to walk away, but the old lady caught his arm. 'No — stay. Husband and wife must have no secrets between them. I need to put something right, Isla, something I've kept from you for a long time, because I thought it was for the best.'

'Is it about my father?' Isla asked.

Her grandmother caught her hands. 'Yes, love. You see I do know his identity. I've known for a long time but chosen not to tell you. But now I realise I was wrong, and I need to right that wrong before it's too late. Forgiveness is important — remember that, Isla. You loved your Uncle Tom, didn't you?'

Her heart pounded. 'Oh, yes. He was a lovely man and I still miss him.'

'You were always special to him. He and your Aunt Ellen met at Art College, as you know. There was almost four years between your mother and Ellen. Leona was just about to go to college, barely eighteen, when Ellen got married. Tom was helping her with her studies — at least that's what we thought, but later we realised he'd been teaching her other things as well!'

Isla swallowed. 'Are you implying what I think you are, Gran?'

Her grandmother nodded and squeezed Isla's hand so hard that it hurt. Isla sat quietly, not daring to look at Jed as Martha relayed the story.

'So, you are telling me that Uncle Tom is really my father,' Isla breathed, wanting to know the end of the story, now that she knew the beginning.

Her grandmother nodded. 'As you've grown up, it's become more and more apparent that there are similarities between yourself and Tom. You've got his rich brown eyes, the same shaped nose and, above all, his lovely smile that can make the room light up.'

After a few moments, Isla asked the question that was uppermost in her mind.

'Did he know about me being his daughter?'

Her grandmother hesitated. 'I'm sure he must have suspected. He was so very fond of you. Your mother kept the secret from the rest of us until she died. She left a letter with her will. I like to think Tom would have married Leona after he and Ellen divorced, but sadly it wasn't meant to be.'

Jed got up then and, shortly afterwards, returned with some tea.

Isla held onto her grandmother's hand for a long time without saying anything. It had been an emotional afternoon; such a mixture of highs and lows, but Isla was able to assure her grandmother that she was forgiven for keeping the secret.

*   *   *

The church was packed for the wedding of Isla Milne and Jed Rowley the following May. It was a glorious day and Isla, wearing ivory satin, made a radiant bride. The Woodbridge Arts Society was there in full force. Aunty

June was resplendent in purple, with a magnificent hat complete with feather.

The Westfields were well-represented too; Sam and Mollie, James and Julie and their cousin, Tom, a tall, still handsome man in top hat and tails, who had flown all the way from Canada to walk his daughter down the aisle.

To everyone's amazement, Jed's mother, Irene, was there too, from Scotland. But the proudest person in the congregation was Martha Milne, who, determined to see her granddaughter married, had been brought by a carer all the way from Bexhill-on-Sea.

Young Skye, sitting between her mother and Amy Bradshaw, summed it all up when she proclaimed loudly, 'It's a lovely wedding, isn't it? But why are all those men wearing silly hats?'